Bumper Book of

Humphrey's

Ti

Betty G. Birney worked at Disneyland and the Disney Studios, has written many children's television shows and is the author of over forty books, including the bestselling *The World According to Humphrey*, which won the Richard and Judy Children's Book Club Award, as well as a further nine books in the *According to Humphrey* series, and eight books in the *Humphrey's Tiny Tales* series. Her work has won many awards, including an Emmy and three Humanitas Prizes. She lives in America with her husband.

Praise for Humphrey:

'Humphrey, a delightful, irresistible character, is big-hearted, observant and creative, and his experiences . . . range from comedic to touching.' *Booklist*

'This is simply good-good-good.' *Kirkus Reviews*

'Children fall for Humphrey, and you can't beat him for feelgood life lessons.' *Sunday Times*

Bumper Book of Humphrey's Tiny Tales

Betty G. Birney

Illustrated by Penny Dann

FABER & FABER

First published in this collection in 2014
by Faber and Faber Limited
Bloomsbury House, 74–77
Great Russell Street, London WC1B 3DA

Printed in England by CPI Group (UK) Ltd, Croydon CR0 4YY

A CIP record for this book
is available from the British Library

ISBN 978–0–571–31049–4

6 8 10 9 7 5

Welcome to MY WORLD

Hi! I'm Humphrey. I'm lucky to be the classroom hamster in Room 26 of Longfellow School. It's a big job because I have to go home with a different student each weekend and try to help my friends. Luckily, my cage has a lock-that-doesn't-lock, so I can get out and have BIG-BIG-BIG adventures!

CONTENTS

My Mixed-Up
MAGIC TRICK!

I'd like you to meet some of my friends

Og

a frog, is the other classroom pet in Room 26. He makes a funny sound: BOING!

Golden-Miranda

has golden hair, like I do. She also has a dog named Clem. Eeek!

Mrs Brisbane

is our teacher. She really understands her students – even me!

Lower-Your-Voice-A.J.

has a loud voice and calls me Humphrey Dumpty.

I-Heard-That-Kirk

LOVES-LOVES-LOVES to joke and have fun.

Repeat-It-Please-Richie

is Aldo's nephew and a classmate of mine.

Stop-Giggling-Gail

loves to giggle – and so do I!

Speak-Up-Sayeh

is unsqueakably clever, but she's shy and doesn't like to speak in class.

I think you'll like my other friends, too, such as *Wait-For-The-Bell-Garth*, *Sit-Still Seth* and *Pay-Attention-Art*.

CONTENTS

Homework

I've learned about a lot of things in my job as classroom hamster.

I've learned about reading, writing, maths, history and science.

I've also learned about art and music.

Oh, yes, and I've also learned a lot about *homework*.

7

You see, my classmates work hard in Room 26.

But they also work hard outside of Room 26, when our teacher, Mrs Brisbane, gives them work to do at home.

I don't have to hand in my homework, but I do it anyway.

I work out the maths problems and learn to spell new words in a little notebook I keep hidden behind the mirror in my cage.

But one day, Mrs Brisbane gave us a special homework assignment.

'Class, I want you to choose a job you think you'd like to do when you grow up,' she said.

'Did you say a *job*?' Repeat-It-Please-Richie asked.

'That's right,' Mrs Brisbane replied. 'Find out what it takes to be good at that job and write a three-page report about it. Next Monday, you'll share your report with the class. And I want you to come dressed as a person who does that job.'

This assignment caused quite a buzz.

'When I grow up, I'm going to be

a footballer!' Lower-Your-Voice-A.J. announced. 'And you can all cheer for me.'

'It depends on what team you play for,' Garth said.

Sit-Still-Seth leaped out of his seat. 'I want to be a doctor and help sick people get well,' he said.

'Good for you, Seth!' I squeaked.

I know that all he heard was SQUEAK-SQUEAK-SQUEAK but at least he could tell how much I liked the idea.

The other classroom pet, Og the frog, agreed.

'BOING-BOING!' he said in his funny, twangy voice.

'*I'm* going to be a teacher just like Mrs Brisbane,' Stop-Giggling-Gail said.

It was hard to imagine a teacher giggling as much as Gail does, but her classroom would always be fun.

'I'm going to be a comedian,' Kirk said. 'Here's a joke: Why did the teacher wear sunglasses in class?'

'I don't know, Kirk. Why?' Mrs Brisbane replied.

'Because her class was so bright!' Kirk laughed.

Mrs Brisbane laughed, too. 'I'm sure you will be a comedian, Kirk. And you're right, I do have a bright group of students.'

Then she turned to the class.

'You have a lot of good ideas, so just remember that the report is due on Monday,' she said. 'And come in costume!'

'How are we supposed to know what we want to do?' Richie asked. 'I'm not grown up yet.'

Mrs Brisbane smiled. 'That's true. You'll probably change your mind a few times before you do grow up. But it's still fun to think about things you'd like to do. Don't you have any ideas?'

Richie thought for a few seconds. 'I might be a chef because I like to eat. Or I might be a police officer and put bad guys in jail,' he said. 'Or, I might be an Olympic runner. I'm pretty fast.'

13

I tried to picture Richie all grown-up, dressed in a police uniform, running down a track, carrying a tray of yummy food.

'Those are all good ideas, Richie,' Mrs Brisbane said. 'Just pick *one* for your report.'

When the final bell rang and my classmates hurried out of the classroom, I heard Sayeh ask Golden-Miranda what she wanted to be when she grows up.

'I'll tell you later,' Miranda answered. 'But I don't think anyone else will have the same idea.'

She had a funny smile on her face that made me unsqueakably curious about what she was thinking.

Once Og and I were alone in Room 26, I jiggled the lock-that-doesn't-lock on my cage and scurried over to his tank.

'Og, I already have a job as a classroom pet. So do you,' I told him.

'BOING-BOING-*BOING*!' Og replied.

'But if I couldn't be a classroom pet, could I do another job?' I wondered.

Og didn't answer. Instead, he dived into the water side of his cage and began to splash.

I ducked out of the way because we hamsters don't like to get wet.

Then I scurried back to my cage.

I took out the notebook and pencil I keep hidden behind the mirror and wrote:

JOBS I COULD DO
(besides being the classroom pet):

I didn't write anything else, because I wasn't sure *what* jobs a hamster could do.

Of course, instead of being a classroom pet, I could be a child's pet. Many hamsters have that job

and their families love them. So I
scribbled:

Family Pet

Then I sat and thought some more.

My whiskers wiggled.

My tail twitched.

But I couldn't think of a single
other job for a hamster.

And then I remembered that Mrs
Brisbane's husband once took me
to a place called Maycrest Manor
where I entertained the humans
staying there.

They were people who were
recovering from illnesses or accidents.

And I have to say, I really cheered
them up! So I wrote down:

Cheering-up Hamster

I thought some more.

There must be MANY-MANY-MANY jobs for a clever and curious hamster like me.

After all, I sometimes follow clues to sort out what problems my friends are having so I can help them. So I wrote:

Hamster Detective

And I sometimes
spin, leap, twirl and
whirl to entertain my
friends. They really
enjoy seeing me roll
around the room in my
hamster ball or hanging
from the tippy-top of my cage.

So I wrote:

Hamster Entertainer

I stared at those words for a few
minutes. They just didn't
seem right.

So I changed it.

Hamster ~~Entertainer~~ Star

I looked at my list and I was unsqueakably proud! Although I never want to leave my job as a classroom pet, it was nice to know that I had choices.

And it was also nice to know that I had made a good start on my homework!

Magic-Miranda

Sometimes, when my classmates are outside at break, I take a little nap.

So the next day, I was burrowed down into my bedding, dozing, when I heard voices near my cage.

'It is *too* a real job!' That was Golden-Miranda speaking.

She was speaking much louder than usual.

Miranda Golden is a favourite friend of mine.

I love her curly golden hair. It reminds me of my nice golden fur. That's why I call her Golden-Miranda.

I like everything about her, except for her dog, Clem.

He has sharp teeth and very bad breath!

'It's not a job like a firefighter. Or a footballer!' That was A.J.'s loud voice.

I poked my head out of my bedding.

A.J. was standing in front of Miranda with his arms folded.

'It's the job I'm doing when I grow up,' she said.

A.J. shook his head. 'Even if it is a job, *girls* don't do it.'

'What job?' I squeaked, but I don't think anyone heard me.

Then Speak-Up-Sayeh appeared at Miranda's side. 'Of course women do that job,' she said in her soft voice.

'Maybe,' A.J. agreed. 'But none of them are famous.'

Pay-Attention-Art must have been paying attention, because he joined in.

'A.J.'s right,' he said.

Then Miranda looked REALLY-REALLY-REALLY angry.

Something was terribly wrong! I hopped out of my bedding and climbed up the side of my cage.

'Mrs Brisbane! Where are you?' I squeaked at the top of my tiny lungs.

Just then, our teacher rushed over and asked, 'Will someone please tell me what you're arguing about?'

A.J. pointed to Miranda. '*She* picked a job that's not a real job. And even if it happened to be a real job, girls don't do it.'

Miranda pointed to A.J. 'He's *wrong.*'

'Calm down, both of you,' Mrs Brisbane said. 'What job do you want to do, Miranda?'

Miranda glared at A.J. 'I'm going to be a magician. I'm going to be a *great* magician. And I really mean it!'

'Of course you do,' Mrs Brisbane said. 'Because it is a real job. There are people who make a living doing magic acts.'

A.J. shook his head. 'I never saw a girl do magic.'

'Of course girls – and women – are magicians,' Mrs Brisbane told him.

'Name one famous girl magician,' A.J. said.

Mrs Brisbane thought for a moment. 'I don't know the names of many magicians. There was Houdini, of course. He was a great escape artist a long time ago.'

'If Houdini was still alive, what would he be?' Kirk asked.

Before anyone could answer, Kirk said, 'The oldest person in the world!'

Everybody laughed, except for A.J.

'But Houdini was a *man*,' he said.

'Maybe Miranda will be the first famous female magician,' Mrs Brisbane told him.

'I'll show you, A.J.,' Miranda said.

'YES-YES-YES!' I squeaked.

The bell rang and all my friends went to their desks.

I didn't hear anything about magic for a while, because Mrs Brisbane sent my friends to the library.

'Take your notebooks,' she reminded them as they headed out of the door. 'You'll want to find out as much as you can about your jobs.'

Mrs Brisbane left with the rest of the class.

When we were alone, I turned towards Og's tank.

'I'm unsqueakably good at escaping from my cage,' I said. 'Like

that magician called Houdini.'

'BOING-BOING!' Og hopped up and down.

I sighed. 'I may be the best hamster escape artist in the world, but nobody knows it ... except you.'

Og dived into the water in his tank and splashed loudly.

I grabbed the notebook and pencil hidden behind my mirror.

Quickly, I added something to the list of jobs I could do.

Escape Artist

I made sure my notebook was safely back in its place when the class returned to Room 26.

'I think you got a good start on your reports,' Mrs Brisbane said. 'But don't forget, I want you to come dressed for your job when you present your report on Monday. And bring as many props as you'd like.'

Sayeh shyly raised her hand. 'Mrs Brisbane, would it be all right if I used Humphrey for my report?'

'Of course, Sayeh,' Mrs Brisbane said.

'No!' Miranda exclaimed. 'I'm planning to use Humphrey! I signed up to take him home for the weekend so we can practise. I'm sorry, Sayeh, but it's really important.'

Sayeh looked VERY-VERY-VERY disappointed.

'Could one of you use Og?' Mrs Brisbane asked.

Sayeh suddenly looked happier. 'Yes! I'd love Og to help me.'

I was unsqueakably happy to see Sayeh smile.

Og hopped up and down. 'BOING-BOING!' he said.

All afternoon, I wondered what tricks Miranda and I would perform

together in her
magic act.

Would she pull me
out of a hat?

It's dark and stuffy
inside a hat.

Would she turn me
into a frog?

I think one frog is
enough for Room
26. And I like being
a hamster!

Would she saw
me in half? Once I
saw a magician
on TV saw a
woman in half.

(Luckily, he put her back together again.)

'NO–NO–NO!' I squeaked. 'Please don't saw me in half! I'm already really small!'

Some of my classmates began to giggle.

'Humphrey sounds very excited about being in your presentation,' Mrs Brisbane said.

Then I remembered Miranda's terrible dog, Clem.

His breath is awful and he hangs around my cage.

And I'm *pawsitive* he doesn't hang around my cage because he wants to be friends!

Just thinking about Clem makes me shiver and quiver.

'I'm not excited,' I shouted. 'I'm scared!'

My friends just giggled again, because all they heard was SQUEAK-SQUEAK-SQUEAK.

Later that night, I took out my little notebook and stared at my list of hamster jobs.

I had a few new ideas. The first one was:

Report Helper

Then I had another idea. My paw shook a little as I thought about Clem's large teeth. I wrote:

Dog Toy

I didn't sleep a wink that night. Not one wink.

Disappearing Act

Of course, I was nervous when I got to Miranda's house on Friday afternoon.

But Clem was nowhere to be seen.

'Humphrey, my mum sent Clem to Gran's house for the weekend so he wouldn't bother you,' Miranda announced.

I felt MUCH-MUCH-MUCH

better. In fact, I felt so much better, I slept like a baby that night.

'I have a lot of work to do this weekend,' Miranda said as she set my cage on the desk the next morning.

'And I need your help,' she added.

'I'm ready!' I squeaked.

'First, I have to look like a magician,' Miranda said.

She disappeared into her wardrobe.

When she came out again, she was wearing a black jacket with long sleeves and a tall black hat.

'Ta-da!' she said. 'I'm now Magic-Miranda.'

I always call her Golden-Miranda because of her golden hair.

But she looked like Magic-
Miranda with the hat on.

Miranda pulled a small table
covered with a black cloth to the
centre of the room.

There was a big box on the table.

'This is my magic table,' she said.

She opened the box and pulled out a wand.

'Every magician needs a magic wand,' she said.

'Of course,' I agreed.

Next, Miranda opened my cage and gently took me out.

She set me on the table and placed books around the edge, so I wouldn't fall off.

Then she said, 'Humphrey! What have you got in your ear?'

'My ear? Nothing!' I squeaked.

Like all hamsters, I store food in my cheek pouches, but I don't put *anything* in my ear.

She reached one hand towards my ear.

'Why, look!' she said. 'It's 10p!'

She held up a small, silver coin.

'Eeek!' I squeaked.

It didn't seem possible.

Hamsters don't have much use for money.

And my ear is much too small to hold 10p!

Miranda stroked my back with her finger and laughed.

'Don't worry, Humphrey,' she said. 'It wasn't really in your ear. It's a trick.'

That made me feel a LOT-LOT-LOT better.

'My Uncle Wally used to pull coins out of my ear when I was little,' she said. 'When I got older, he taught me the trick.'

I wondered how Miranda did that.

'I had the coin hidden in my hand all the time,' she said. 'But it took a lot of practice before I could make it work.'

She did the trick again, but this time she showed me how she had the 10p hidden in her hand all the time.

'It takes a lot of practice to learn a magic trick,' Miranda explained. 'I probably tried this a hundred times.'

I was unsqueakably impressed!

'You can help me with the next trick,' she said.

Miranda opened the box and took out a pack of cards.

She separated the pack into two piles and told me, 'This is called shuffling. It's a way to mix up the cards so no one knows where any card is in the pack.'

After she shuffled them together really fast using her thumbs, Miranda set the pack of cards in front of me and spread them out, face down.

Humans have amazing thumbs!

'Pick a card,' she said. 'Any card.'

I moved forward a few steps and sniffed one of the cards.

It didn't have much of a smell, so I moved along.

One of the
cards smelled
a little bit like
berries.

I don't know
why a card
would smell like
berries. Maybe
someone was
playing a card
game and eating
berries at the
same time.

I headed
for the berry-
smelling card and
scratched at it.

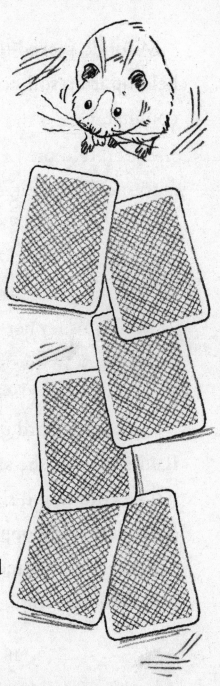

Miranda picked the card up and held up it up so I could see it, but she couldn't.

'This is the card you picked. Remember it,' she said.

The card had a six in one corner and a six in the opposite corner.

There were six red hearts in the middle of the card.

'Got it?' Miranda asked.

I squeaked.

She put the six of hearts back with the other cards.

'I'll cut the pack in half,' she said.

I watched carefully as Miranda split the pack into two piles. Then she put it back together.

I tried to figure out where my card went, but the backs of the cards all looked alike.

Then Miranda spread the cards on the table face up.

A few seconds later, she picked up a card and said, 'Here's your card.'

It *was* my card – the six of hearts!

How did she do that?

'It's not magic,' she said. 'There's a secret to it.'

I begged her to tell me the secret, but I guess all she heard was SQUEAK–SQUEAK–SQUEAK.

Miranda reached into the box again and pulled out a paper cup.

While she held the cup in one hand, she pulled a small wooden bead out of her box.

'Now I'll show you the vanishing bead trick,' she said. 'Watch closely.'

'I will!' I squeaked.

Miranda dropped the bead into the cup.

Then she picked up her magic wand and waved it over the cup.

'Abracadabra –
abracaday, make the
bead go away,' she said.
She set the wand
back on the table and turned the cup
upside down.

I was unsqueakably
surprised when the
bead didn't tumble out!

Where could it have gone?

'There's no bead in the cup,'
Miranda said.

Then she reached into
her pocket. 'Because the
bead is *here*.'

She pulled the bead
out of her pocket.

She really was Magic-Miranda!

'Wow!' I squeaked. 'How did you do that?'

Miranda bowed.

'There's one important rule for magic,' she said. 'Don't *ever* answer questions about a trick.'

I was unsqueakably disappointed.

'But since you're going to be my assistant, I'll tell you how I did it,' Miranda told me.

Oh, it was a clever trick!

First, there were two matching beads. One of them was in her pocket all the time!

Second, there was a hole in the bottom of the cup, which she had hidden from me.

So when she turned the cup over, the bead dropped into her hand so it couldn't fall out.

It was a very tricky trick!

Miranda showed me more tricks.

She made a pencil stick to her hand without anything holding it on!

Then she made a spoon bend and then brought it back to its normal shape.

I couldn't figure out how she did those things and she didn't tell me.

Late in the afternoon, Miranda's mum came in to see how we were doing.

'Miranda, I hope you haven't worn Humphrey out,' she said. 'After all, this is his day off from school.'

'He's going to be my assistant,' Miranda said.

'That's a good idea,' her mum said. 'But I hope you don't make Humphrey disappear.'

Miranda had a playful grin on her face. 'No, but I'm going to make *A.J.* disappear!'

'NO-NO-NO!' I said.

I was pretty sure that Miranda would get into a lot of trouble if she made A.J. disappear.

What would his family think?

Miranda set up her table and then sat behind it, facing her mum and my cage.

In front of her was an upside-down glass and a piece of paper made into a tube.

She picked it up to show us that it was completely open inside.

Next, she held up a photo.

'Here's A.J.,' she said. 'This was from his birthday party.'

Miranda put the photo on the table. 'And now, I'm going to make him disappear.'

She placed the paper tube over the glass so we couldn't see the glass at all.

Then she put the glass on top of the photo, so we couldn't see it any more.

'Presto-changeo,' Miranda said as she slid the glass across the table.

I still couldn't see the photo because it was under the glass.

Miranda took the paper tube off the glass. 'No more A.J.'

I could see the glass, but the photo of A.J. was gone!

Miranda's mum clapped her hands. 'Wonderful! Now can you bring him back?'

Miranda nodded. She put the paper around the glass and slid it across the table.

'Hocus-pocus!' Miranda lifted the glass and the photo was back!

Miranda was REALLY-REALLY-REALLY magic!

The Amazing
Humphrini

On Sunday, Miranda and I practised
most of the day.

She began to include me in the act.

'My assistant, the Amazing
Humphrini, will now select a card,'
she said when she did the card trick.

Amazing Humphrini! That name
made me feel like a real magician.

'After you pick the card, I'll ask

someone from the audience to come forward and take it and memorise what it is,' she explained.

'Great!' I squeaked.

She did the vanishing bead act and just before she pulled the second bead out of her pocket, she looked at me and said, 'Where do you think the bead has gone, Humphrini?'

I squeaked and she said, 'You're right! It's in my pocket.'

It was HARD-HARD-HARD work, but I knew the class would love Magic-Miranda's act.

Monday morning was unsqueakably exciting in Room 26.

It was amazing to see all my friends in their costumes.

A.J. wore his football kit and Seth wore a white jacket, like a doctor.

Gail had dressed like Mrs Brisbane with a short grey wig.

I couldn't wait to see what Richie wore, because he'd had so much trouble deciding what he wanted to be when he grew up.

To my surprise, he wasn't dressed like a police officer, an Olympic runner *or* a chef.

Instead, he wore a suit and tie!

'What are you going to be when you grow up, Richie?' Mrs Brisbane asked.

'I'm going to be a banker and have piles and piles of money!' he said.

Just before the bell rang, I turned to my neighbour, Og. 'If Miranda calls me Humphrini, it's all right,' I told him. 'That's my magician's name.'

'BOING-BOING!' Og yelled as he hopped up and down.

Mrs Brisbane began the reports right away.

Stop-Giggling-Gail didn't giggle once when she explained how teachers like Mrs Brisbane worked hard to make sure that their students learned things that would help them grow and be successful.

A.J. explained how much practice

and training went into
becoming a top footballer.

He also showed some
remarkable moves, kicking
the ball around the room.

Speak-Up-Sayeh told us that when she grew up, she wanted to be a vet and take care of all kinds of animals, from horses to frogs and hamsters!

As always, Sayeh spoke softly.

'I would like to be a vet, because I love maths and science and I love animals,' she said. 'A vet makes sick animals better and does things to help healthy animals stay healthy.'

'Go, Sayeh!' My friends all laughed at my squeaking.

Then she walked over to Og's cage and told us the things she had learned about caring for frogs.

'A frog that jumps a lot is a healthy frog,' she said.

Og jumped all around the land
side of his tank. 'BOING-BOING-
BOING-BOING!'

Everyone laughed and so did I.

I was HAPPY-HAPPY-HAPPY
that Og was healthy.

The reports went on.

I didn't understand everything

Richie said when he explained something called 'interest' on money, but I found his talk very *interest*ing'.

Kirk told a lot of funny jokes when he talked about being a comedian.

My favourite joke was when he said, 'Did I tell you about the day my brother found carrots growing out of his ears?'

He paused and then said, 'Boy, was he surprised! He'd planted radishes!'

When everyone stopped laughing, Kirk explained that the last part that makes you laugh is called the *punch line*.

Seth wore a white coat, because he wanted to be a doctor for humans.

He showed us how to take a pulse and talked about yucky things called germs.

The morning flew by and it was soon time for lunch.

Mrs Brisbane let Miranda prepare her magic act while everyone was out of the room.

I watched as she carefully set up a table with the black cloth and put books around the edges.

She made sure that the cards, the coin, the paper cup, the glass, the magic wand and all the things she needed were in the box.

She carefully put one of the wooden beads in her pocket.

Then she and
Mrs Brisbane left
to go to lunch.
'Wait until you
see her act,' I told
Og. 'She really is
Magic-Miranda!'

Og seemed
very excited as he
splashed around
in the water.

And then I saw
it: the wooden
bead.

It was on the
floor, near the leg
of the table.

I couldn't believe my eyes! It must have fallen out of Miranda's pocket.

She'd be unsqueakably upset when she reached for it and it was gone.

I glanced at the clock. Eeek!

The students would be coming back any minute.

But if I hurried, I could get the bead back on to the table without getting caught outside my cage.

I jiggled my lock-that-doesn't-lock and raced across the table.

'I've got something important to do,' I squeaked to Og as I ran past his tank.

I slid down the leg of the table and headed straight for the bead.

'BOING–BOING!' Og said.

'I'm hurrying, Og,' I told him.

I knew I'd need both paws to get back up to my cage, so I tucked the bead in my cheek pouch, where I store food.

It didn't taste very good, I'm sorry to squeak.

I scurried back to the table and grabbed the cord hanging down from the blinds.

Using all my might, I began to swing on the

cord, going HIGHER-HIGHER-
HIGHER until I reached the table top.

Then I let go of the cord and
landed on the table, near Og's tank.

Just then the door to Room 26
opened and my friends rushed into
the room.

I dashed into my cage and pulled
the door behind me.

Luckily, no one saw me outside
my cage.

That was a good thing!

But I still had the bead in my
cheek pouch.

That was a bad thing!

Miranda had on her black jacket
and top hat and began her act.

'I am Magic-Miranda,' she said.

My mind was racing as Miranda pulled a coin out of Richie's ear.

'How'd you do that?' he asked as my friends all laughed.

But Miranda didn't tell him.

Then she did the trick where the pencil stuck to her hand.

(I'll tell you a secret. It didn't really stick there. She was holding it with the other hand, but I didn't notice it.)

And the trick where she bent the spoon.

(I'll tell you a secret. She didn't really bend it, but it looked as if she had.)

Everyone clapped.

Then she took me out of my cage and put me on the table.

'Here is my assistant, the Amazing Humphrini,' she said.

Everyone clapped again. But all I could think about was the bead in my cheek pouch.

Magic-Miranda began her card

trick and when she spread the cards
out and told me to pick one, I did.

She asked Mrs Brisbane to look at
the card and remember it.

This time the card had pictures of
three black diamonds in the middle.

And that's the same card Miranda
pulled out after shuffling the cards
again.

Even Mrs Brisbane was impressed with that trick!

I thought she'd do the vanishing bead trick next, but instead, she announced that she would make A.J. disappear.

'I don't believe it,' he said.

'You'll see.' Miranda took out the photo of A.J., which made everyone laugh.

But my friends weren't laughing when she put the photo under the glass and made it disappear.

(At least it *looked* as if it disappeared.)

Everyone gasped.

And A.J. looked HAPPY-HAPPY-

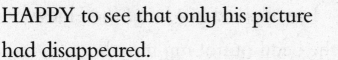

HAPPY to see that only his picture had disappeared.

Miranda had saved the bead trick for last.

I know Miranda thought everyone would be surprised when she pulled the bead out of her pocket.

But I knew that *Miranda* would be the one surprised when the bead wasn't there.

She placed the bead in the cup and turned it upside down.

When the bead didn't fall out of the cup, everyone gasped.

Miranda reached into her pocket.

I saw the look of horror on her face when she realised the bead wasn't there!

I swallowed hard and then blew
the bead out of my mouth.

It rolled across the table and
stopped right in the middle.

At first, the room was silent.

Then everyone began to cheer!

My friends were clearly amazed.

'How'd she do that?' I heard Heidi
ask Gail.

Miranda took a bow and pointed
to me.

'Thank you, Amazing Humphrini,'
she said.

When the class was quiet again, Mrs Brisbane told Miranda she was a wonderful magician.

'But I don't think it's a good idea to put a bead in a hamster's mouth,' she said.

She was right about that!

'But I didn't! I thought it was in my pocket,' Miranda explained. '*That* was truly magic.'

At the end of the day, Miranda came over to my cage and thanked me.

'I'll never figure out how you got that bead,' she said. 'But you really are amazing, Humphrini!'

A.J. rushed up to Miranda. 'Those

tricks were great,' he said. 'Could you teach them to me sometime?'

'Sure,' Miranda said. 'As long as you don't mind learning magic from a girl.'

I was glad when A.J. smiled and said, 'I guess I was wrong about girl magicians.'

That night, when things were quiet in Room 26, I took out my little notebook and pencil and looked at my list.

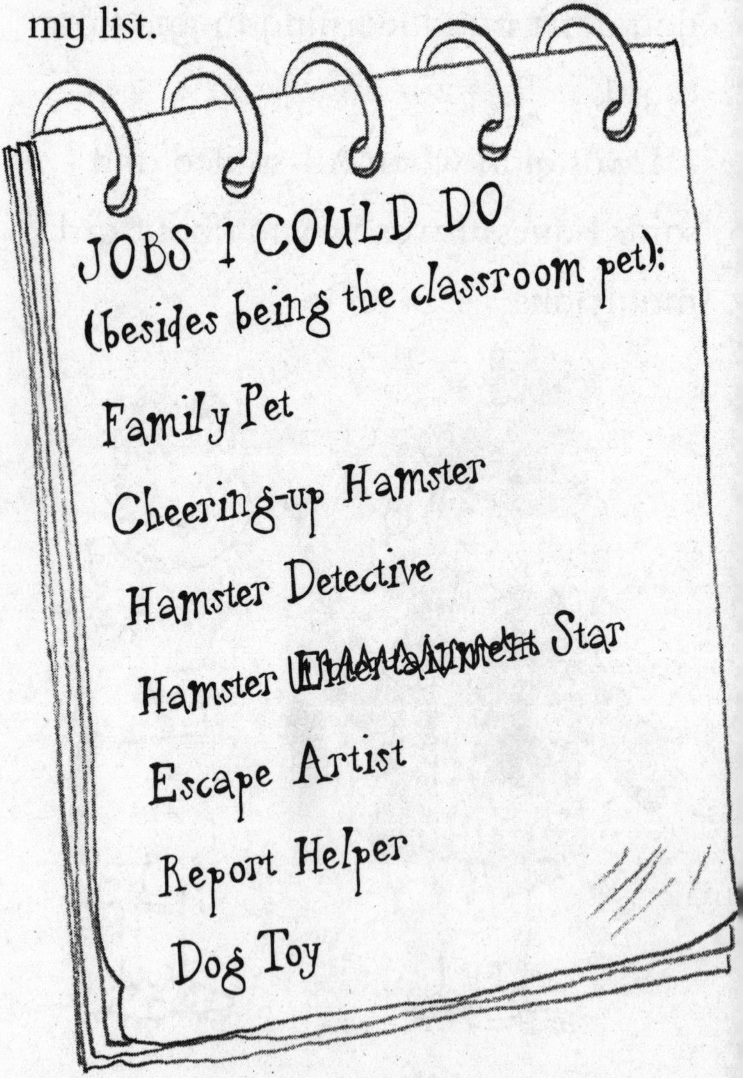

JOBS I COULD DO
(besides being the classroom pet):

Family Pet

Cheering-up Hamster

Hamster Detective

Hamster ~~Entertainment~~ Star

Escape Artist

Report Helper

Dog Toy

Then I added something new:

Hamster Magician (The Amazing Humphrini)

'You know what, Og?' I squeaked to my neighbour. 'There are a lot of jobs a hamster like me could do.'

'BOING-BOING-BOING!' he agreed.

'But I still think being a classroom pet is the very best job of all,' I said.

And I knew I was right.

Magic Trick

How to Make Things Disappear

(Coins, Cards, Photos)

Golden-Miranda says that magicians *never* share their secrets, but she told me how she made A.J.'s photo disappear. It's unsqueakably clever and you can do it, too! Turn the page to see how.

Things you need:

A table covered with something white or black.

A large piece of paper, any colour or pattern.

A clear glass with a rim wide enough to cover whatever you want to disappear.

Scissors.

Glue.

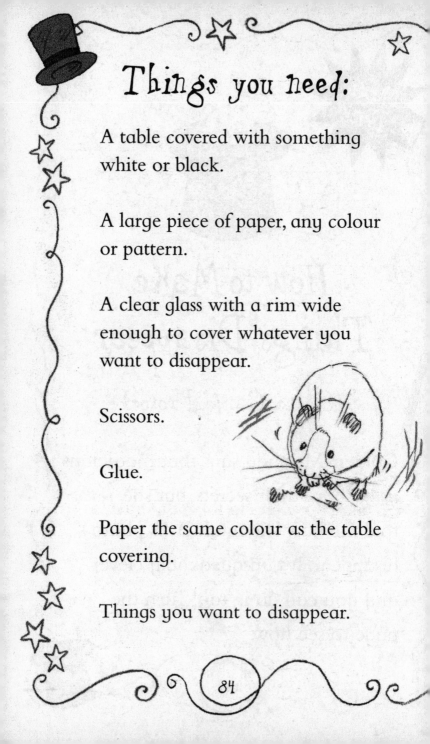

Paper the same colour as the table covering.

Things you want to disappear.

Getting ready

1 Cut the large piece of paper to make a tube that fits around the glass. It shouldn't fit too tightly and it should be taller than the glass.

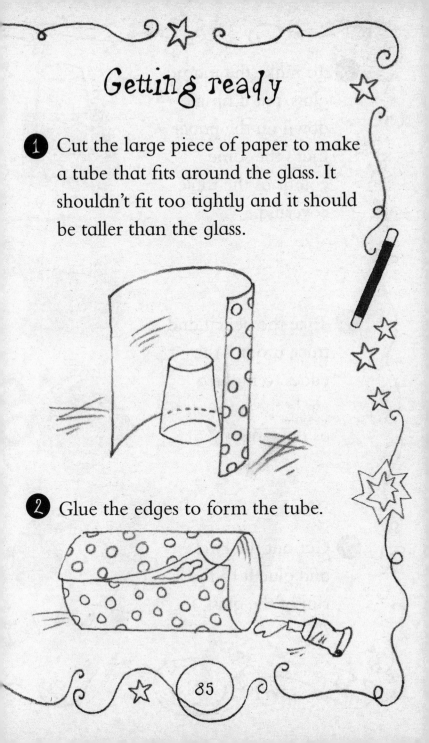

2 Glue the edges to form the tube.

3 To make the magic glass, put it upside down on the paper that's the same colour as the table covering.

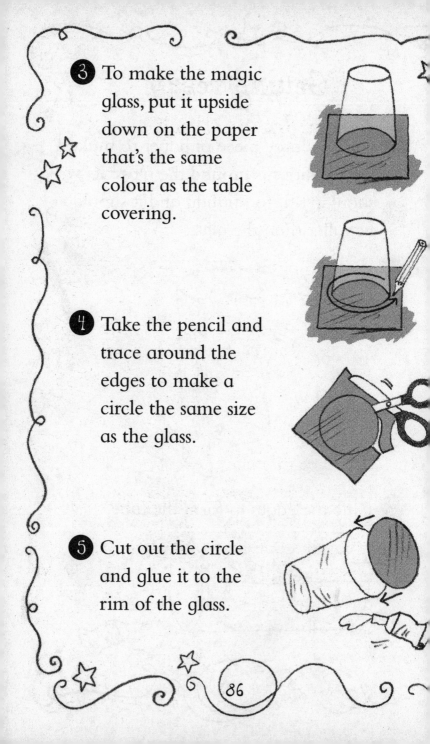

4 Take the pencil and trace around the edges to make a circle the same size as the glass.

5 Cut out the circle and glue it to the rim of the glass.

Now you're ready to do the trick!

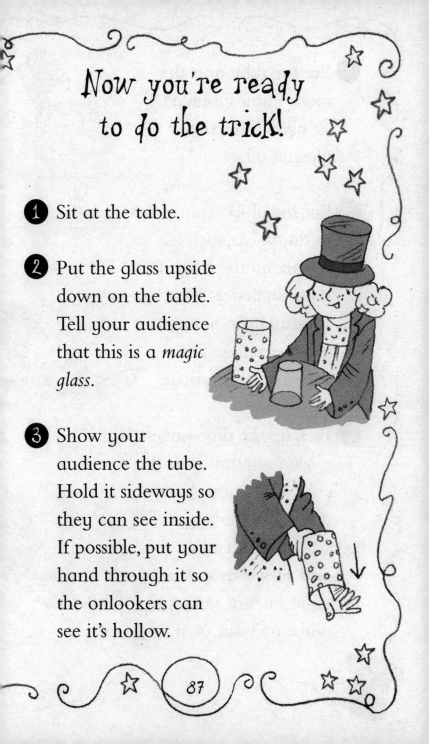

1 Sit at the table.

2 Put the glass upside down on the table. Tell your audience that this is a *magic glass*.

3 Show your audience the tube. Hold it sideways so they can see inside. If possible, put your hand through it so the onlookers can see it's hollow.

4 Put the tube over the glass – you shouldn't be able to see the glass at all.

5 Put the object you want to disappear, such as a coin, on the table. Tell your audience, 'This is a coin and I'm going to use the magic glass to make it disappear.'

6 Pick up the tube-covered glass and put it over the coin. Wave your hands and say some magic words. 'Abracadabra' and 'Hocus-pocus' are good ones or you can make up your own.

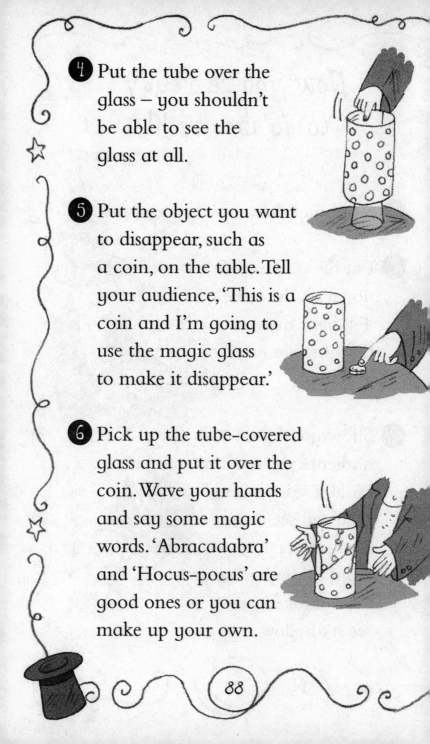

7 Lift the tube off the glass. It will look as if the coin has disappeared, because the paper glued to the glass will hide it. Tell your audience, 'See? The coin has disappeared.'

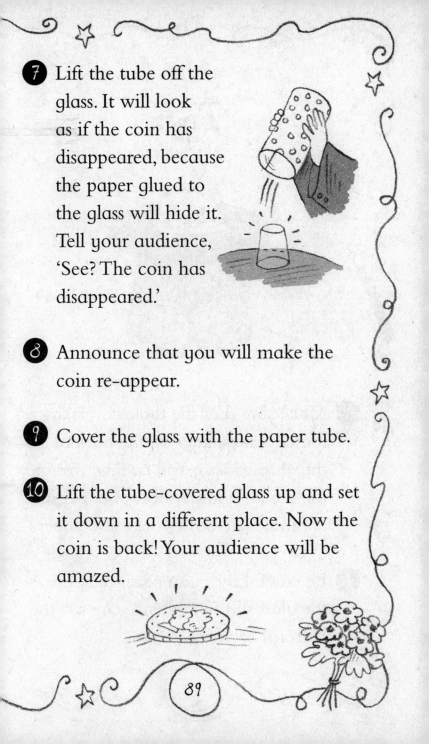

8 Announce that you will make the coin re-appear.

9 Cover the glass with the paper tube.

10 Lift the tube-covered glass up and set it down in a different place. Now the coin is back! Your audience will be amazed.

Tips:

1 Make sure that the table covering matches the paper on the bottom of the glass exactly. You could cover the table with a large sheet of paper and cut the circle out of the same paper.

2 Be careful that you never pick up the glass so the audience can see the bottom.

3 Remember to pick the glass straight up.

4 Don't slide it.

5 Don't forget, all tricks take LOTS-LOTS-LOTS of practice, so don't give up easily.

My Pet Show
PANIC!

I'd like you to meet some of my friends

Og

a frog, is the other classroom pet in Room 26. He makes a funny sound: BOING!

Mrs Brisbane

is our teacher. She really understands her students – even me!

Lower-Your-Voice-A.J.

has a loud voice and calls me Humphrey Dumpty.

Wait-For-The-Bell Garth

is A.J.'s best friend and a good friend of mine, too.

Speak-Up-Sayeh
is unsqueakably smart, but she's shy and doesn't like to speak in class.

Golden-Miranda
has golden hair, like I do. She also has a dog named Clem. Eeek!

Don't-Complain-Mandy
has a hamster named Winky!

Grandma Grace
is A.J.'s grandmother. She LOVES-LOVES-LOVES hats!

I think you'll like my other friends, too, such as *Repeat-It-Please-Richie, Pay-Attention-Art, Raise-Your-Hand-Heidi* and *Sit-Still-Seth*.

CONTENTS

I Go to the
Pet Show

'Hang on, Humphrey,' A.J. said.

The car his mum was driving turned a corner and I slid across my cage.

'I'm trying!' I squeaked back.

Car rides aren't easy for hamsters like me.

I don't even have a seat belt.

I'm the classroom hamster in

Room 26 of
Longfellow School.

I get to ride in cars a lot because
I go home with a different student
each weekend.

'This is my lucky day,' A.J. told me.
'Mrs Brisbane picked me to bring
you home for the weekend. So I get
to take you to the Pet Show.'

A.J. and I had both been excited

when Mrs Brisbane told us about the Pet Show.

'This is your lucky day, too,' A.J. told me. 'You're going to win a prize!'

I crossed my paws and hoped he was right.

'Remember, A.J., Humphrey might not win,' A.J.'s mum said.

'There are lots of prizes,' A.J. explained. 'He's sure to win one of them. And I get to keep it!'

'Don't you have to share it with the class?' A.J.'s mum asked.

'Humphrey's my pet,' A.J. said. 'At least for the weekend.'

He pulled out a paper and read to his mum while she drove.

'Here are the prizes,' he said, reading the list out loud.

Most Friendly
Best Trick
Most Unusual
Longest Tail
Biggest Ears
Loudest Voice
Best in Show

Just then my tummy jiggled and joggled.

Was that because of the bumpy road?

Or was it because I was worried that I might not win a prize?

I didn't want to let down my
friends in Room 26. After all, they
were counting on me to win.

A.J.'s Grandma Grace leaned over
and looked in my cage.

'He's one fine-looking hamster,' she
said.

'Thanks a lot!' I said. But like most humans, I'm sure all she heard was 'SQUEAK-SQUEAK-SQUEAK.'

I liked Grandma Grace.

I liked Grandma's Grace's purple hat, too.

When the car stopped, I slid across the floor of my cage.

'We're here,' A.J.'s mum said.

'Yay!' A.J. shouted.

'Yay!' his younger brother Ty shouted.

'Yay!' his

younger sister DeeLee shouted.

'Goo!' his baby brother shouted.

'Eek!' I squeaked quietly.

*

The Pet Show was in a big building in the middle of the park.

Outside, it was nice and quiet.

Inside, it was NOISY-NOISY-NOISY. And what noises there were!

Barking, meowing, chirping, snarling!

Yipping, yapping, squealing, shouting!

Someone called out, 'Quiet, please!' But it still wasn't quiet.

'Here you go, Humphrey Dumpty,' A.J. said as he set my cage on a table.

I like it when A.J. calls me Humphrey Dumpty.

I call him Lower-Your-Voice-A.J.

because his voice is so loud. I have special names for all my friends in Room 26.

While A.J.'s family went to see the other pets, I looked around the room.

There was a lot to see, like dogs on leashes and cats in cages.

There was a lot to hear, like a screeching sound that made my whiskers wiggle and my tail twitch.

'BAWK!' a voice said. 'Crackers is pretty!'

I wondered what kind of creature was such a screecher.

Next, a soft voice said, 'Hi, A.J.'

I looked up and saw Sayeh from Room 26. I call her Speak-Up-

Sayeh because she is VERY-VERY-
VERY quiet.

'Hi!' A.J.'s voice boomed.

Sayeh put a glass tank down next
to me on the table.

'Og!' I squeaked.

I was unsqueakably happy to see
my friend Og.

'Mrs Brisbane said I could bring him,' Sayeh said. 'I hope he wins a prize, too.'

'BOING!' Og said.

He makes a very funny sound. He can't help it. He's a frog.

He's also my neighbour back in Room 26. His tank, which is half water and half land, sits right next to my cage.

Next, A.J.'s best friend Garth showed up.

I call him Wait-For-The-Bell Garth because he's always the first one out of the door at the end of the day. He said he had come to see me win a prize.

'Okay,' A.J. said. 'But I'm the

one who keeps the prize because I
brought Humphrey.'

Another friend, Don't-Complain-
Mandy, arrived with her pet hamster,
Winky. Mandy's in Room 26, too.
She doesn't complain much since she
got Winky.

'I think Winky will
win Most Friendly,'
she said.

'I just hope one

of us
wins a prize,' Winky
squeaked to me from
his cage.

'Me, too,' I said.
Winky is one of my

friendliest friends, so I meant it. But I still didn't want to let A.J. down.

Richie showed up with a box with holes in the sides. Mrs Brisbane always asks him to repeat his answers in class, so I call him Repeat-It-Please-Richie.

'Hi, everybody!' he said. 'Want to see my new pet?'

'I do!' I squeaked.

A.J., Garth and Sayeh gathered round as Richie took the lid off the box.

'Meet Nick,' Richie said.

Garth's eyes opened wide. 'Wow!' he said.

'That's amazing!' A.J. said.

'Amazing,' Sayeh whispered.

What made Nick so amazing? All I could see was a box.

Richie put the box down next to me so that my cage was between the box and Og's tank.

I climbed up my ladder to get a better view, but all I could see were some leaves and twigs.

Was Nick invisible? Or had he escaped?

'There's nothing there,' I squeaked down to Og.

'BOING-BOING!' Og sounded disappointed, too.

I was pretty sure that leaves and twigs couldn't win a prize at the Pet Show.

But I still wasn't sure I could win one, either.

The Show
Begins

'The Pet Show is about to begin,' a
voice said.

I looked up at the stage and was
surprised to see Carl was speaking.
Carl worked at Pet-O-Rama, the
shop where I lived before I came to
Room 26.

'Hi, Carl!' I squeaked.

He couldn't hear me over the

yipping, yapping, screeching and snarling.

'Bawk! Crackers will win!' the screecher said. 'Bawk!'

I was already pretty sure Crackers would win the prize for Loudest Voice.

Carl introduced the judges for the Pet Show.

The first judge was Ginger Jones. She was a pet groomer from Pet-O-Rama.

She smiled and waved to the crowd.

The second judge
was Stormy Smith.
He was the weather
man from TV.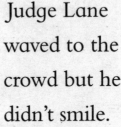

He smiled and
waved to the
crowd.

The third
judge was a real judge. A Justice of
the Peace.

Judge Lane
waved to the
crowd but he
didn't smile.

Then the
judges went to
look at the cats.

I heard a lot
of meowing,
growling
and hissing,
which was
unsqueakably scary
for a small hamster
like me!

Richie leaned down and spoke to Nick.

'Don't worry, Nick. You're sure to win,' he said.

Who was this Nick, anyway? Why was Richie so sure he would win?

'Og, maybe if I got up higher I could see him,' I said.

I scrambled to the top of my ladder, jumped onto my tree branch and climbed up to the very top.

Then I carefully got up on my tip-toes and grabbed the top bars of the cage.

Paw over paw, I worked my way to the corner. When I looked down, I felt a little dizzy, but maybe I would

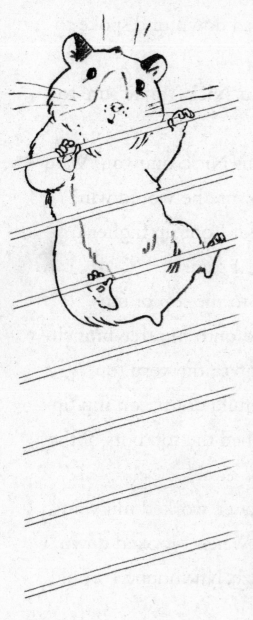

win the prize for Best Trick!

But after all that climbing, all I saw was that pile of old leaves and twigs in the box next to my cage.

Was Richie playing a trick on the judges?

'There's still nothing there, Og,' I squeaked to my friend.

Og splashed around in the water in his tank, but I knew he was disappointed.

'And now, the Parade of Pooches,' Carl announced.

The owners brought their dogs out to the centre of the room. Luckily, they were on leashes. I must admit, I've been a bit afraid of dogs ever since I came nose-to-nose with an unsqueakably rude one named Clem.

The dogs and their humans walked around in a circle while Carl introduced them.

One dog named Oscar was

LONG-LONG-LONG but his legs
were SHORT-SHORT-SHORT. He
looked like a giant hot dog. Carl said
he was a dachshund.

Then there was a tall, spotted dog
named Smoky, who held his head
high. He walked when his human

walked and stopped when his human
stopped.

When his owner said, 'Heel,'
Smoky followed right at her heels.
Good dog!

Next came a teeny-tiny dog
named Cha-Cha. She walked very

fast to keep up with her human.

Doodles was a shaggy dog with no eyes at all. At least I couldn't see any under all that fur. But he seemed to know where he was going. Then my heart went THUMPITY-THUMP-THUMP.

I didn't need to hear Carl say the next dog's name. I'd know that big nose anywhere!

It was Miranda's dog, Clem. I love Golden-Miranda. That's what I call her, but her name is really Miranda

Golden. She is one of my favourite friends from Room 26.

I didn't love Clem. I'd met him when I spent a weekend at Miranda's house.

I still remembered his large, sharp teeth and his smelly doggy breath.

As Miranda led him around the

circle, the judges made notes.

'Next, the other pets,' Carl announced.

Other pets? Did that mean Og and me?

'Bawk! Crackers will win!' a voice screeched.

I hopped on my wheel and started spinning.

'The judges are coming, Og,' I told my friend. 'Be friendly, splash around, make some noise!'

I didn't hear a thing coming from his cage.

Why was Og so quiet? Didn't he want to win a prize? Did he want to let our friends down?

The judges walked towards the table.

'Remember, we're here to win, Og,' I squeaked. 'It's showtime!'

First, the judges looked at a creature called a bearded dragon. Eeek!

I thought dragons breathed fire and ate people. But this dragon

turned out to be a fancy lizard
named Lola.

'She's very unusual,' Stormy Smith
said.

'Very,' Ginger Jones agreed.

'Hmm,' Judge Lane said as he
made notes.

Then the judges looked at a guinea

pig, a turtle and a rabbit named Peter.

Next, they moved to my friend Winky's cage. Winky was born with one eye closed, so he always looked as if he was winking.

'Wow, he's friendly,' Ginger Jones said.

'Crackers is pretty! Crackers

will win,' that awful voice
screeched.

Now I could see Crackers,
sitting on her human's arm.
She was a huge bird with
green and yellow feathers.
And she was quite pretty.

'Ah, a parrot,' Judge Lane said, looking at Crackers.

Stormy Smith nodded. 'A fine-looking bird.'

The girl who owned her said, 'Sing, Crackers!'

The crowd all cheered when Crackers sang, 'La–la–la!'

I liked Crackers' singing.

I didn't like her large, sharp beak.

As the judges headed towards our end of the table, my tummy felt jumpy and jiggly again.

I heard Garth tell A.J., 'I know Humphrey's going to win a prize.'

'Of course he will,' A.J. said, but he sounded worried.

Maybe he wasn't really sure I could win.

To squeak the truth, neither was I.

Here Come
the Judges

First, the judges stopped at Og's tank.

'Show them what a great frog you, are, Og,' I told my friend. 'Do your very best.'

Everyone stared at Og.

Og stared back, but he didn't do anything else.

'BOING for them, Oggy!' I squeaked.

But Og didn't BOING. He didn't even splash.

He just stared at the judges. They stared back.

'Come on, Og,' Sayeh whispered. 'Show them what a good swimmer you are.'

Og kept on staring.

What did Og see? I looked out at the crowd.

I saw people, dogs, cats, dragons, birds and other strange creatures.

Maybe Og was scared.

'Don't be afraid, Og,' I said. 'Act friendly. Say hello!'

'BOING!' he said at last.

Stormy Smith looked surprised.
'What was that?' he asked.

'That's how he talks,' Garth
explained.

'BOING-BOING!' Og jumped up
and down.

The judges leaned in and looked interested until Crackers opened her beak and started squawking again.

'Crackers is the best!' she said.

Then Og stopped. He didn't make another sound.

But at least he'd tried. A little.

The judges moved on to my cage. Now it was all up to me.

'Who's this?' Stormy Smith asked.

'Humphrey,' A.J. said. 'He's a golden hamster.'

Unlike Og, I put on a great show.

First, I leaped up to the side of my cage, looked straight at the judges and squeaked hello.

'He's a friendly little fellow!'

Stormy Smith
exclaimed.

Next, I
hopped onto my
wheel and did a
fast spin.

'Look at him
go!' said Ginger
Jones.

I climbed
back up to the
top of my cage,
grabbed the
highest bar, and
swung there by
one paw.

Sometimes, I

amaze myself.

'Goodness,' Judge Lane said.

Next, I slid DOWN-DOWN-DOWN and dropped back onto the wheel. This time, I spun backwards!

My whiskers were wilting, but I kept on spinning as the judges made notes.

'Great job,' said Ginger Jones.

I was unsqueakably proud.

Then she noticed the box next to me.

'What's in there?' she asked.

'That's Nick,' Richie said. 'I'll make him move.'

The judges came closer as Richie poked around inside the box.

I stopped spinning so I could watch.

Even Judge Lane looked surprised. 'I thought it was a stick until it moved,' he said.

I thought I saw a stick move in there, too. But a stick doesn't move all by itself, does it?

'It's a stick insect,' Richie explained.

'That's why I call him Nick – Nick the Stick.'

People crowded round to see Nick.

'The stick is an insect!' I squeaked to Og.

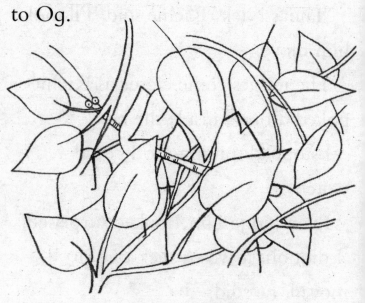

'BOING-BOING!' Og twanged loudly.

He was probably excited because he likes insects.

He likes them for dinner. And breakfast, too. Yuck!

'BOING-BOING-BOING!' Og repeated.

People in the crowd chuckled.

'Og has a pretty loud voice,' A.J. said.

I guess he still hoped that Og could win a prize.

So did I.

Next, Carl asked the owners to bring pets with special tricks to the centre of the room.

Smoky, the spotted dog, rolled over and sat up and begged.

Cha-Cha, the tiny dog, stood on her hind legs and did a hula dance.

At least, that's what her owner called it.

Oscar, the dachshund, sang. It was

more of a wail than singing.

Crackers tried to drown him out by
singing 'La-la-la.'

It was NOISY-NOISY-NOISY.

But I was still wondering what kind of animal a stick insect was. Was it an insect or was it a stick?

Luckily, I have a secret lock-that-doesn't-lock that allows me to get in and out of my cage without humans knowing.

So while everyone watched the tricks, I jiggled the lock and slipped out of my cage.

As the door swung open, I saw Miranda lead Clem to the centre of the room.

I didn't think Clem was clever

enough to do a trick, but it turned
out he could chase his own tail. I was
just glad he wasn't chasing me.

While everyone watched Clem, I
tiptoed over to Nick's box. I couldn't
see over the top, but there were air
holes in the side of the box. I got up
on my tip-toes and peeked inside.

What an unsqueakably strange
sight!

Nick still looked like a stick, but
now I saw that the stick had eyes!
And it moved ever so slowly.

'Eeek!' I squeaked.

I'm sure no one heard me, because
the crowd was cheering.

I looked over and saw that the
people were cheering for a cat.

'I never heard of a cat doing tricks,'
I heard A.J. tell Garth.

'Me neither,' Garth replied.

But this cat did a great trick. His
owner held up a big hoop and the
cat leaped right through it.

Then he turned round and leaped

through it again!

The trick was so amazing I forgot I was out of my cage.

Then something happened that made me forget about Nick the Stick.

I wasn't worried about winning a prize any more.

I was only worried about staying alive!

A Matter of
Life and Breath

When the dogs saw the performing cat, they got excited. I'd never heard so much barking, howling, yipping and yapping in my life.

But Clem was more excited than any of them.

'Down, boy!' Miranda yelled as Clem tugged at his leash.

She tried to stop him, but he pulled

the leash right out of her hand
and rushed towards the cat.
As the cat jumped
through the hoop
again, Clem
jumped right
after him!

Then a
strange thing
happened. Clem
stopped chasing the
cat and he sniffed the
air. I'm not sure what
he smelled, but he headed

straight for me!

That's when I remembered I was out of my cage. And if Clem got to me before I got to my cage, I'd be in big trouble!

Og tried to warn me. 'BOING-BOING-BOING!'

But there wasn't much else he could do.

Just as I reached the cage, I saw Clem's big nose poke up over the edge of the table.

I saw his sharp, shiny teeth.

I smelled his horrible doggy breath.

'Bad dog!' Miranda shouted.

She was right. He was a BAD-BAD-BAD dog!

'Somebody, stop that
dog!' Carl shouted.

'Humphrey's out of the cage!'
A.J. bellowed.

'Grab him!' Garth yelled. 'Quick!'

Before anyone could grab me,
Clem pounced. His jaws opened
wide.

Eeek! I took a flying leap and landed on his long nose.

Clem's eyes crossed as he tried to look at me.

I jumped again and landed between his ears. Clem didn't like that, so he shook his head – hard. I hung on for dear life to a clump of his fur.

Just then, Og leaped up out of his tank, popping the plastic top right off. He landed next to me on top of Clem's head.

Clem seemed VERY-VERY-VERY confused. I don't think he'd ever had a hamster and a frog on his head before.

He lowered his head and shook it again to get us off.

Og and I slid straight down to the floor!

'Run, Og. Hurry!' I squeaked as I raced away from Clem.

My heart was pounding. As we ran and hopped, hopped and ran, there was panic at the Pet Show, but no one was more scared than I was.

'Bad dog! Come back!' That was Miranda.

'Bad-dog – bawk!' That was Crackers.

'Somebody, stop that dog!' That was Carl again.

I could smell Clem's awful doggy breath and knew he was close behind.

Then, everything went dark. The world turned upside down. Og and I were flipped up, down and all around.

'I've got them!' a voice called out.

'Eeek!' I squeaked.

Finally, I could see light again.

'A hat always comes in handy,' Grandma Grace said.

She was smiling down at us. I

didn't know who she was at first, because she wasn't wearing her purple hat.

Then I saw what had happened. Og and I were inside Grandma Grace's hat. She had thrown it over us, then scooped the hat up. That purple hat saved our lives.

'Thanks, Grandma Grace,' I squeaked weakly.

'BOING!' Og sounded pretty tired, too.

Lots of humans gathered round to look at us, but Grandma Grace shooed them away.

'Let these little fellows rest,' she said.

I liked Grandma Grace and her purple hat VERY-VERY-VERY much.

★

I was happy to be back in my cage and to hear Og splashing in his tank.

Then the judges stepped forward and said they had chosen the winners of the prizes.

My tummy did a flip-flop. I hoped my friends wouldn't be too disappointed if I didn't win a prize.

'It was a tough choice,' Stormy Smith said.

'We think you're all winners,' Ginger Jones said.

'Let's hand out the rosettes,' Judge Lane said.

I crossed my toes as they awarded the prizes.

The Best Trick prize went to the cat who jumped through the hoop. His name was Noodles.

Peter the rabbit won the Biggest Ears prize. That was no surprise!

The prize for the Longest Tail went to Clem.

I suppose he did have the longest tail, but I wouldn't have given him a

prize for anything. Still, I was happy for Miranda.

Crackers won the prize for the Loudest Voice.

'Crackers is the best!' the parrot squawked.

She was loud, all right. I just wished that sometimes she'd keep her beak shut.

'There were two winners for Most Unusual Pet,' Stormy Smith said.

My ears pricked up. Maybe Og could get a prize here.

But the two winners were Nick the Stick and Lola the bearded dragon.

Og had lost to a bearded lady and a stick!

I was happy for Richie, though. He jumped up and down and high-fived his friends.

'I'm sure you'll win the next prize, Humphrey,' A.J. whispered to me.

I noticed that A.J. had his fingers crossed, so I crossed my paws as well.

Stormy Smith announced another prize with two winners.

'The prizes for Most Friendly Pet
go to Winky and Humphrey,' he said.
I could hardly believe my tiny ears.

'BOING–BOING!' Og twanged.
Everybody cheered and I was
HAPPY-HAPPY-HAPPY to share
the prize with Winky.

'I won!' A.J. shouted. 'I won a
prize!'

'No, Humphrey won,' Garth said. 'He's the class pet of everybody in Room 26. Why should you get the prize?'

A.J. looked surprised. 'Well, I brought him here, didn't I?'

He leaned down next to my cage. 'Way to go, Humphrey,' he said.

But I thought that not sharing my prize wasn't the way to go at all.

When Mandy and A.J. stepped up to accept the prizes, A.J. asked if he could say something.

Stormy Smith handed A.J. the microphone. Not that A.J. needed one with his loud voice.

'I want to share this prize with

everybody in Room 26,' he said.
'Humphrey's our classroom hamster.
He belongs to us all.'

I was unsqueakably proud of A.J.
for sharing!

The judges gave the prize for Best
in Show to Smoky, the spotted dog.

The crowd cheered and I joined in.

I thought all the prizes had been awarded, but the judges weren't finished.

'We are also giving a very special prize,' Stormy Smith said with a big smile on his face.

'Og the Frog gets the prize for Best Friend, for helping Humphrey.'

Og won a special prize for helping me!

Sayeh looked very proud and so did my other friends from Room 26. Stormy handed the microphone to her.

If there's one thing Sayeh doesn't like, it's speaking in front of other

people. But in her soft voice, she also
shared the prize with everyone in
Room 26.

As the crowd clapped, my friends
started chanting, 'Og, Og, Og, Og!'

No one squeaked louder than I did.

When things quietened down again,
Stormy Smith said, 'We'd also like
to thank Mrs Grace Cook,' he said.
'Thanks for your quick thinking and
your purple hat.'

Grandma Grace waved to the
cheering crowd.

My tiny paws were getting sore
from clapping!

★

'THANKS-THANKS-THANKS for

helping me,' I told Og when the noise died down.

Og dived to the bottom of his tank.

Then he did three backwards somersaults.

It was a prize-winning trick, but no one saw it except me.

Home,
Sweet Home

On the way home, A.J. seemed quieter than usual.

'What's the matter?' asked Grandma Grace. 'You're not usually so quiet.

'I just wish I could get a pet,' he said. 'But Dad says not right now.'

I wished he could, too. He always took GOOD-GOOD-GOOD care of me.

'You already have a great pet,'
Grandma said. 'He's right here in the
car. And he's got a big, shiny rosette!'

A.J. sighed. 'But I have to share
Humphrey with everyone in Room
26.'

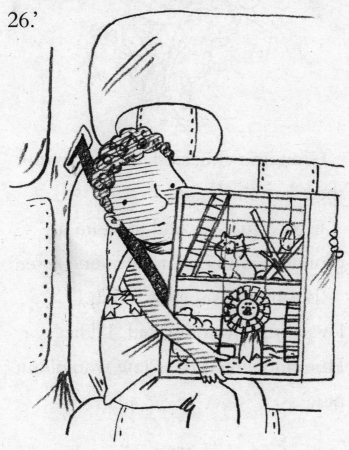

Grandma chuckled. 'You have to share me, too.'

It was true. A.J. had to share his grandma with his brothers and sister.

'But you know how much I love you,' Grandma said. 'I'll bet Humphrey feels the same way about you.'

Grandma Grace was one smart human.

'It's TRUE-TRUE-TRUE,' I squeaked.

A.J. laughed. 'Humphrey Dumpty, you're funny. I wouldn't want any pet but you. And Og, too.'

That made me feel even better than winning a prize at the Pet Show.

★

A.J. couldn't wait for us to go back to school on Monday so he could show my rosette to our teacher, Mrs Brisbane.

He was PROUD-PROUD-PROUD.

So was I.

Everybody wanted to tell Mrs
Brisbane about what had happened
at the Pet Show.

'It was so funny to see that purple
hat running across the floor with
Humphrey and Og
under it,' Garth said.

'It was wonderful,' Mandy said.
'Although it was terrible that
Humphrey was in danger.'

When I heard the word 'danger', I
let out a loud 'Eeek!'

'But it was wonderful that Og was
so brave and helped him,' Mandy
continued.

Miranda looked as if she was about to cry. 'Oh, I feel horrible,' she said. 'My dog could have hurt Humphrey, or worse!' she said. 'I'm so sorry.'

She looked so upset, I felt sorry for her, even if Clem was a truly awful dog.

By the way, doesn't Pet-O-Rama sell breath mints for dogs?

'I hope Humphrey stays in his cage from now on,' Mrs Brisbane said, looking at me. 'I don't want anything bad to happen to you.'

Mrs Brisbane is an unsqueakably smart human.

'Richie, maybe you can bring Nick the Stick in one day for

our biology lesson,' Mrs Brisbane
continued.

'Sure,' said Richie. 'Any time!'

At the end of the day, when all my
friends had gone to their homes, Og
and I were alone in ours – Room 26.

I looked at the shiny rosette
hanging on my cage.

I looked at the shiny rosette
hanging on Og's tank.

'I'm glad we won prizes, Og,' I told
him. 'We made our friends happy.'

Og splashed around in the water.

Then I continued. 'But I don't
really need a prize because being
a classroom pet is the BEST-BEST-
BEST job in the world!'

'BOING-BOING-BOING!' Og
twanged.

Even though I don't really
understand frog talk, I was pretty
sure that he agreed with me.

My Summer Fair SURPRISE!

I'd like you to meet some of my friends

Og

a frog, is the other classroom pet in Room 26. He makes a funny sound: BOING!

Mrs Brisbane

is our teacher. She really understands her students – even me!

Lower-Your-Voice-A.J.

has a loud voice and calls me Humphrey Dumpty.

Wait-For-The-Bell-Garth

is A.J.'s best friend and a good friend of mine, too.

Golden-Miranda

has golden hair, like I do. She also has a dog named Clem. Eeek!

Speak-Up-Sayeh

is unsqueakably smart, but she's shy and doesn't like to speak in class.

Aldo Amato

is a grown-up who cleans Room 26 at night. He's a special friend who always brings me a treat and seems to understand my squeaks better than most humans.

Repeat-It-Please-Richie

is Aldo's nephew and a classmate of mine.

I think you'll like my other friends, too, such as
*Stop-Giggling-Gail, Pay-Attention-Art,
Raise-Your-Hand-Heidi* and *Sit-Still-Seth*.

CONTENTS

Surprising News

I've learned a lot about school in the short time I've lived in one.

As a classroom hamster, I get to see and hear everything that goes on in Room 26.

One thing I've learned is that it's important to listen to our teacher.

Mrs Brisbane is unsqueakably smart. She's a good teacher, too.

I've also learned that it's important to listen to the headmaster, Mr Morales.

Mr Morales is the Most Important Person at Longfellow School.

One Monday when he came into our classroom, he said something *very* important.

It was also quite surprising.

'As you know, class, the Longfellow School Summer Fair is coming up on Saturday,' he said.

My friends got very excited.

'WILL THERE BE CAKE?' A.J. asked.

A.J.'s voice is very loud, so I call him Lower-Your-Voice-A.J.

Mr Morales said there would be cake.

There would also be games and crafts and things that sounded like FUN-FUN-FUN.

'Yippee!' I shouted.

Of course, all that my friends heard was a very loud 'Squeak!'

'This year, we're trying to raise money for new playground equipment. We're adding something new,' Mr Morales said. 'And you will all be part of it.'

'Are you listening, Og?' I squeaked to my neighbour.

Og is a frog. He lives in a tank right next to my cage on a long table by the window.

Since I can't see his ears, I'm never sure if he's listening or not.

'BOING-BOING!' he answered in his funny voice.

I guess he was listening after all.

'The students in each room are going to do a project about what they like best about their class. Everyone will make posters and banners,' Mr Morales explained.

'Oooh,' my classmates said.

'Then, in the afternoon, all classes will parade their banners around the school field,' Mr Morales said. 'There will be a prize for the best class presentation.'

'Ahhh,' my classmates said.

'Do you think Room 26 will win?' Mrs Brisbane asked the class.

Every student shouted 'Yes!' including me.

After Mr Morales left, Mrs Brisbane talked to the class about maths.

I was so excited, I hopped on my wheel for a fast spin.

I should have listened to Mrs Brisbane, but all I could think about was the fair.

'It sounds exciting, doesn't it, Og?' I asked when we were alone during breaktime.

'BOING-BOING!' Og answered.

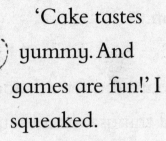

'Cake tastes yummy. And games are fun!' I squeaked.

'BOING-BOING-BOING!' Og agreed.

'I just have one question, Og. Do you think Room 26 will win the prize?' I asked.

Og dived into the water and splashed loudly.

I guess he wasn't sure.

I wasn't sure, either. But I knew we'd find out VERY-VERY-VERY soon.

★

I heard my friends say some very odd things when they came back from break.

'Coconuts,' Garth said.

Gail giggled and said, 'Sponges!'

Stop-Giggling-Gail loves to giggle, but I had never heard her laugh about sponges before.

Sayeh, who I call Speak-Up-Sayeh because she hardly ever speaks, smiled and said, 'Face painting!'

Face painting – what was that?

I hoped she was talking about paintings *of* faces.

Painting *on* faces would be VERY-VERY-VERY messy.

Especially on a hamster.

'Class, it's time to start our project,' Mrs Brisbane announced.

'We need to think about our posters. What do you like best about our class?' she asked.

Lots of hands went up.

'We learn a lot of important things in Room 26,' Mandy said.

I had to agree with that.

I've even learned to read and write in Room 26, which is unusual for a hamster.

'We've got the best teacher,' Richie said.

192

That made Mrs Brisbane smile.

'But other classes have good teachers and learn a lot. Any other ideas?' she asked.

I looked around the room.

I liked the unsqueakably nice bulletin board with pictures of important people on it.

I didn't know who the people were, but I was sure they were important.

I looked around some more and saw books, pencils, paper and maps.

My friends glanced around the room, too.

Then Miranda Golden raised her hand. I think of her as Golden-Miranda because of her golden hair.

'We have the nicest students,' she said with a smile. 'And the best friends.'

She was RIGHT-RIGHT-RIGHT! I was lucky to be in a class with such nice humans. 'I agree,' Mrs Brisbane said.

Suddenly, Heidi said, 'I like
Humphrey and Og!'

(Heidi doesn't always remember to
raise her hand before speaking. That's
why I call her Raise-Your-Hand-
Heidi.)

Then A.J. shouted, 'They're what I

like best about Room 26!'

Suddenly, the class was buzzing with excitement.

Mrs Brisbane clapped her hands to quieten everyone down.

'Quiet, please,' she said. 'I agree. Humphrey and Og make this class very special. We could put pictures of them on our posters for the parade.'

My classmates all cheered but I was too surprised to squeak up.

I've been a classroom hamster for quite a while.

But I'd NEVER–NEVER–NEVER had my picture on a parade poster before.

*

On Tuesday, Mrs Brisbane gave each
student a large piece of cardboard.

'It's time to start making our
posters,' she said.

My friends all went to work
drawing and writing on the blank
pieces of cardboard.

They couldn't finish them in one day, because they still had lessons to do as well.

So the next day, Wednesday, they worked on the signs again.

By the end of the day, I could finally see what they had done.

Richie's sign read: *Room 26 is hamster-iffic!*

Art's sign read: *Room 26 is frog-tastic!*

I think they meant that Og and I were terrific and fantastic.

That made me feel GOOD-GOOD-GOOD.

There were other great signs, too. Miranda's read: *Humphrey rules!*

Sayeh's sign said: *Go, Og!* That's funny, because Og is 'go' spelled backwards.

Tabitha and Kirk made signs that read: *Hamster Power* and *Frogs Rule!*

The signs were every colour of the rainbow.

Some had flowers and glitter.

Some had funny pictures of Og and me.

All of them made me proud to be in Room 26!

★

The next day, after science, my friends made ears.

YES–YES–YES! They took paper, scissors, crayon and glue and made little hats with hamster ears sticking up.

It was unsqueakably funny to see my human friends wearing hamster ears.

(They didn't make frog ears because, as I said, frogs don't have ears that you can see.)

'You've done a wonderful job,' Mrs Brisbane told the class. 'Tomorrow we'll practise our marching.'

★

I didn't wait until the next day to work on my marching.

Once my classmates had gone home, I started to practise.

'One-two-three-four.' I marched across my cage.

'One-two-three-four.' I marched back across my cage again.

I heard Og splashing around in his tank.

Splashing was not like marching.

But frogs weren't like hamsters, either.

★

'Aldo's here to bring you cheer!' a friendly voice said later that evening.

Aldo, the school caretaker, wheeled his cleaning trolley into the room.

'How are my favourite classroom pets?' he asked.

'Unsqueakably fine!' I answered.

'BOING!' Og said.

Aldo glanced around the room and saw Richie's jacket still draped over his chair.

'Oh-oh. Richie forgot his jacket,' he said. 'I'll have to talk to him about that.'

Aldo happens to be Richie's uncle.

As usual, Aldo went right to work. While he swept and dusted, he talked to us.

'Guess what, fellows?' he asked.

'What?' I squeaked back.

'I'm going to be in the wet-sponge booth for the fair,' he said.

I was squeakless.

Gail had said something about sponges. But what on earth was a wet-sponge booth?

'Yep. People pay money to throw wet sponges at some of the folks who work at the school,' he said. 'I think even Mr Morales is going to have sponges thrown at him.'

I couldn't imagine anyone throwing a sponge at the headmaster *or* the caretaker.

'Anything to help make money for the new playground equipment,' he said.

I could see his point, but I hoped no one would throw a wet sponge at me. After all, hamsters should NEVER–NEVER–NEVER get wet!

Og probably wouldn't mind, since he spent half his time in the watery part of his tank.

When Aldo finished cleaning, I

practised marching some more.

I didn't know much about fairs, but I knew one thing: I was going to be unsqueakably good at marching!

It's Not Fair!

On Friday, Mrs Brisbane announced that it was time to finish the signs for the parade. She had brought long sticks so the students could hold them up.

Once the sticks were attached to the signs, my friends marched around the classroom, carrying them.

'One-two-three-four,' I squeaked as

I marched across my cage.

'The signs look wonderful,' Mrs Brisbane said. 'Hold them high.'

'Shouldn't we do something else?' Raise-Your-Hand-Heidi said.

'Like what?' Mrs Brisbane asked.

Heidi wasn't sure but Speak-Up-Sayeh had an idea.

'We could say something about Room 26,' she said softly.

Garth said, 'Yeah. Something about Humphrey and Og.'

That idea got my whiskers wiggling!

Soon, all my

friends were making up sayings about Room 26.

Humphrey-Humphrey, Og-Og!
We've got a hamster and a frog!'
And:
BOING-BOING, SQUEAK-
SQUEAK,
Humphrey and Og – hear them speak!
But they finally decided on:
Humphrey and Og are so much fun,
They make our classroom number 1!

★

My friends marched around the classroom again, chanting about Og and me.

I was so excited, I squeaked along with them.

Humphrey and Og are so much fun,
They make our classroom number 1!

It was paw-sitively thrilling!

Mrs Brisbane finally stopped the

marching and my friends sat back

down.

'Thank you for such good work,' she said. 'At the fair tomorrow, you can have fun with your friends and families until 2 p.m. Then we'll all meet by the bouncy castle and line up for the parade.'

A castle that bounces? How could that be?

Garth raised his hand. 'Who will bring Humphrey and Og?' he asked.

Mrs Brisbane looked surprised.

'Bring them where?' she said.

'Bring them out for the parade,' Garth said.

Mandy, Miranda and Richie all raised their hands and offered to bring us.

Mrs Brisbane shook her head.

'I'm sorry,' she said. 'Humphrey and Og can't be in the parade. It would be too dangerous.'

I could see how sorry my friends were. But no one was more disappointed than I was.

Og dived down into the bottom of his tank. I think he was upset, too.

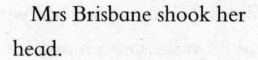

Golden-Miranda asked why it would be dangerous.

Mrs Brisbane explained that I was too small to march in a parade and if someone carried me, I might get hurt.

She said that Og certainly couldn't march and he needed to be near water.

She also said that it was going to be a hot, sunny day. The hot sun is not good for hamsters or for frogs.

Everything she said was true, but I still felt SAD-SAD-SAD.

So did my friends.

'Maybe we could pull them in a trolley,' Garth suggested.

Now that was an unsqueakably
good idea!

'There's still the sun,' Mrs
Brisbane said. 'I would worry about
Humphrey and Og.'

'They could wear hats,' Stop-
Giggling-Gail said. Then she giggled.

Everyone else giggled, too.

I guess a hamster would look
pretty funny wearing a hat.

'I know!' Mandy said. 'He could have an umbrella.'

Everyone giggled at the thought of a hamster holding an umbrella, too.

'I'm sorry,' Mrs Brisbane said. 'I don't think Humphrey and Og can be in the parade. But everyone will know about them because of your signs.'

She moved on to talking about

maps and faraway places.

I moved on to thinking about the fair.

The fair I would never ever see.

★

I always look forward to going home with a different student each weekend.

So I was surprised when Mrs Brisbane told me I would spend the night in the classroom.

'Everyone in class will be coming to the fair tomorrow morning,' she said. 'You'd be left alone all day in someone's house if they took you home tonight. After the fair, I'll take you to my house.'

I was still disappointed I wouldn't
be going to the fair.

But I'd had lots of good times at
the Brisbanes' house.

'Fine with me!' I squeaked.

★

Aldo came back to clean that night.

I didn't even know he cleaned on
Friday nights!

'Humphrey and
Og, I'm glad to
see you,' he said.
'Because tonight, I
have lots to do.'
Aldo always has
a lot to do. But that
night, he worked so

fast it made my head spin.

When the room was clean, he said,
'I'm not finished yet.'

Then he began to behave very
strangely.

First, Aldo measured my cage.
He'd never done that before.

Next, he measured Og's tank.
He certainly hadn't done that
before.

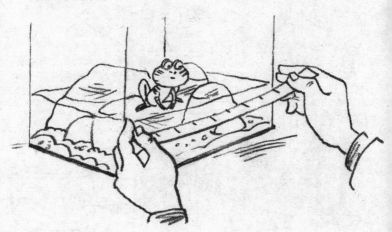

'Aldo, what are you doing?' I squeaked.

'Hang on, Humphrey,' he answered. 'You'll find out what's going on soon enough.'

Aldo measured the top of his cleaning trolley.

He made some notes on a piece of paper.

'Great,' he said. 'Everything will be finished in time for the fair tomorrow.'

'WHAT-WHAT-WHAT are you squeaking about?' I asked.

Aldo didn't answer. He wheeled his cleaning trolley out the door.

'What was that all about, Og?' I asked.

Og didn't answer. I guess he didn't know either.

Humans often did odd things.

But the fair made humans act even stranger than usual!

My BIG-BIG-BIG Surprise

The next morning, I woke up in Room 26. But it wasn't like any school day I'd ever known.

First, when Mrs Brisbane unlocked the door, her husband was with her.

'I can't wait to show you the posters,' she told him.

While Mrs Brisbane went to get them, Mr Brisbane rolled his

wheelchair over to see Og and me.

'Hi, fellows,' he said.

'Good morning,' I squeaked.

When Mr Brisbane saw the signs, he said my friends had done a great job.

'Yes,' Mrs Brisbane said. 'But they'll be disappointed if they don't win.'

Mr Brisbane tried on a hamster-ear hat and looked unsqueakably funny.

Next, A.J. and Garth

rushed in. They were SO-SO-SO excited.

'Richie said to meet him here,' A.J. said. 'He said it was important.'

'I haven't seen him yet,' Mrs Brisbane told him.

Sayeh and Miranda hurried into the room.

'Richie said to meet him here,' Miranda said. 'He said he had something to show us.'

Soon, most of my classmates were in Room 26, all looking for Richie.

But Richie still wasn't there.

'I hope he comes soon,' Mandy said. 'I don't want to miss the face painting.'

Just as everyone was about to give

up, the door opened and Richie
entered.

Aldo was right behind him, pushing
his cleaning trolley.

Did Aldo clean on Saturdays, too?

'Wait till you see what Uncle Aldo
made,' Richie said.

Everyone gathered around Aldo and
the trolley, even Mr and Mrs Brisbane.

Of course, I couldn't see very well from the table by the window.

I climbed up to the tippy-top of my cage to get a better look.

'I thought of a way that Humphrey and Og can march with you,' Aldo said.

'Really?' I squeaked.

'Would you like to see how?' Aldo asked.

'Oh, yes,' Mrs Brisbane said, and everyone agreed.

Aldo came over to the window and picked up my cage.

'I'll be careful with you, Humphrey.'

He gently placed my cage on a board he put across the top of the trolley. He set my cage in slots on the board.

'I fixed it so his cage won't slide around,' Aldo said.

'Very clever,' Mr Brisbane said, and everyone agreed.

Next, Aldo got Og's tank and put it in another set of slots on the board.

'Og's tank will stay firmly in place,' Aldo said.

'BOING!' Og said. He sounded very happy.

'Yes, but what about the hot sun?' Mrs Brisbane asked.

Aldo took out a big umbrella and put the handle in another slot on the board.

'They'll be in shade the whole time,' he said. 'What do you think?'

Of course, my friends thought it was a GREAT-GREAT-GREAT idea.

But Mrs Brisbane was the teacher. It was up to her.

'I think it will be fine for Humphrey and Og to march with us,' she said. 'Thank you, Aldo.'

'THANKS-THANKS-THANKS, Aldo!' I squeaked.

Everybody laughed.

'I think we're ready for the fair,' Mrs Brisbane said.

He was right. I was READY-READY-READY to go.

★

The hallway whizzed by us as Aldo rolled the trolley down the hall.

Mr Brisbane rolled along next to us.

'Hey, Og, we're going to the fair!' I
squeaked.

I could hardly believe it.

Aldo rolled us through the
doorway, out to the playground.

231

I'd only seen the playground once before.

I'd seen swings and a slide and lots of open space.

But today, the playground looked completely different.

'What do you think, fellows?' Aldo asked as he pushed us through the crowd.

What did I think? I thought it was amazing!

The open space was filled with people and the most wonderful sights I'd ever seen.

I looked to my right and saw Garth throwing balls at a row of coconuts.

One of the balls knocked the
coconut off its base and everybody
cheered.

'Yay, Garth!' I squeaked.

I doubt if anyone heard me over
all the other noise.

I looked to my right and saw a

table filled with cakes of every size,
shape and colour. Yum!

We moved along and I saw a huge
green castle with children bouncing
up and down inside.

'That must be the bouncy castle,' I
said. 'It looks like fun, doesn't it, Og?'

Og just stared at the crowds with
his big frog eyes.

Mrs Brisbane came up with a

small tiger by her side.

At least I thought it was a tiger.

But it turned out to be Sayeh,
painted to look like a tiger.

'I got my face painted,' she said
with a happy smile.

I still wasn't interested in getting
my face painted.

But it would be fun to be a tiger, at least for a day.

Aldo said he had to go to the wet-sponge booth, so Mrs Brisbane said she'd push the trolley.

'I don't want to miss this,' she said.

She wheeled us past more booths and tables, with games and yummy things to eat.

There was a big crowd gathered around the next booth.

Everyone was laughing at something. But I couldn't see what it was.

'I'll have a look, Og,' I shouted to my friend.

I climbed up to the tippy-top of

my cage, where I hung from one paw.

I saw a big board with a hole in it. Sticking out through the hole was Mr Morales's head!

I was astonished to see my friend, Golden-Miranda, toss a wet sponge right at his face.

Splat! The sponge hit him in the forehead and water rolled down Mr Morales's face.

I was SHOCKED-SHOCKED-SHOCKED that anyone would treat the headmaster like that.

Especially a nice girl like Miranda.

But the most amazing part was that Mr Morales was laughing!

'Who's next?' he shouted.

'It's all for a good cause. We're raising money for new playground equipment.'

So what looked like a very bad thing turned out to be a very good thing.

'Should I give it a try?' Mrs Brisbane asked.

'Sure,' Mr Brisbane answered. 'He said it's for a good cause.'

I never thought I'd see the day

when my teacher would throw a wet sponge at my headmaster. But she did.

As the crowd cheered, she pulled her arm back and let the sponge fly.

It hit him right on the nose.

Everybody laughed. Mr Morales laughed the loudest.

Summer fairs were fun, all right.

They were also very surprising.

1 Surprise Everybody

Mr Morales had to leave the booth to get ready for the parade. Aldo took his place.

The first person to buy a ticket to throw a sponge was Richie.

He pulled his arm way back and threw it at his uncle.

Splat! It hit Aldo on the side of his head.

He laughed so hard, his moustache shook.

'You can do better than that, Richie,' he said. 'Try again.'

Meanwhile, Mrs Brisbane went to get the signs for our class.

She left Miranda in charge of Og and me.

'It's almost time, Humphrey,'
Miranda said as she wheeled us
towards the bouncy castle.

I watched all the children bouncing
around inside.

My tummy felt a little bouncy, too.

Soon Mrs Brisbane was back,
handing out signs to all my friends.

'Look at me, Humphrey,' someone
said.

I looked up and saw a giant
hamster. Eeek!

'It's me – Seth,'
the giant hamster
said. 'I had my
face painted like a
hamster!'

I was HAPPY-HAPPY-HAPPY to see that it really was Seth.

'Look at me,' another voice said.

I looked up and saw a huge green face.

'It's me – Tabitha,' the green face said. 'I had my face painted like a frog!'

'BOING-BOING!' Og said. He sounded quite pleased.

My classmates were all lined up now, holding their signs.

They looked unsqueakably fine wearing their hamster-ear hats.

Mrs Brisbane told the students to

march in two straight lines, holding
their signs high.

'When we get to the stage,
A.J., you lead the chant,' she said.
'Everyone will be able to hear you.'

She asked Miranda and Richie to
push the trolley together.

'I've got an idea,' Richie said.

I couldn't hear what it was because
he whispered it to Miranda.

As the classes lined up, I saw
children carrying all kinds of
colourful signs and banners.

My tummy did a flip-flop. Would Room 26 be the best after all?

'Eek!' I squeaked.

But no one could hear me because a band began to play loud music.

'All right, students. Forward, march!' Mrs Brisbane said.

The trolley lurched forward.

'Og, we're in a parade!' I told my froggy friend.

'BOING-BOING-BOING-BOING!' he replied.

As we marched along, mums and dads, brothers, sisters and grandparents waved at us and cheered us on.

'Signs high! Here we go, A.J.!' Mrs Brisbane said.

We stopped marching when we
reached a wooden stage on the edge
of the playing field.

'Okay, Humphrey,' Richie said.
'I've got a plan for you that will

surprise everybody. Even Mrs
Brisbane doesn't know.'

   I was surprised when he opened
the door to my cage.

   I was surprised when he pulled my

hamster ball out of his backpack and put me inside.

Richie set my hamster ball on the ground.

'Now you can march, Humphrey,' he said.

Mrs Brisbane looked surprised, too.

'Richie!' she said. 'I don't think that's a good idea.'

I looked UP–UP–UP and saw Mr Morales and some other people sitting on the stage, watching.

I heard A.J.'s loud voice lead the others.

Humphrey and Og are so much fun,
They make our classroom number 1!

They sounded great.

I sat in my hamster ball, listening.

'Go, Humphrey, go!' Richie yelled.

I'd forgotten he'd told me to march.

I took a few steps forward, which made my ball spin.

'Go, Humphrey, go!' the whole class shouted.

'No, Humphrey, no!' Mrs Brisbane said.

I suddenly hit a little slope and my ball rolled a little faster.

'Go, Humphrey, go!' the whole crowd yelled.

The slope got steeper and steeper.

My ball rolled faster and faster.

Large feet moved out of the way to let me pass as I rolled along.

I was moving FAST-FAST-FAST. Faster than I'd ever gone before.

'Whoa, Humphrey! Come back!' Richie shouted.

I heard footsteps running behind me.

My ball just kept on going.

'Stop, Humphrey, stop!' I heard the crowd yell.

I looked back and saw people running after me.

All of my classmates were running and yelling.

So were Mrs Brisbane and Mr Morales.

Mr Brisbane's wheelchair was almost flying.

It looked as if everyone at the fair was chasing after me.

I wanted to stop, but a hamster ball doesn't have brakes. I stopped running but the ball kept spinning. And I was spinning with it!

I rolled and rolled and rolled some more.

The trees and grass were just a blur.

I wondered how far a hamster ball could roll. Could it go on for ever?

'Come back, Humphrey!' A.J. shouted.

If I could have come back, I surely
would, because now I saw I was
rolling right toward the car park!

My heart was beating THUMPITY-
THUMP-THUMP when, all of a
sudden, the ball stopped.

It stopped so quickly, I did a triple
flip.

When I'd settled down, I looked up.

A huge foot was right on top of my
hamster ball!

Then a huge hand reached down
and picked the ball up.

'Who have we got here?' the man
holding the ball said.

By then, the crowd had caught up
with me.

I heard Mrs Brisbane's voice say,

'Thank you for saving Humphrey, Officer Jones.'

A huge eye looked down at my hamster ball.

'I should probably give this hamster a ticket for speeding,' Police Officer Jones said. 'But I'll let him go with a warning this time.'

Everybody laughed, except me.

I was way too tired to laugh.

Richie came running up. He looked VERY-VERY-VERY worried.

'Richie, what were you thinking?' Mrs Brisbane asked.

'I'm sorry. I didn't think the ball would roll away,' he said.

Then he looked down at me. 'I'm so

sorry, Humphrey. I made a big mistake.
I wouldn't want anything bad to
happen to you.'

I don't want anything bad to
happen to me, either. But I know
Richie would never want to hurt me.

*

Mrs Brisbane took me back to the
stage.

Mr Morales and all my friends
were waiting there.

'This has been a very surprising
fair,' Mr Morales announced.

That was TRUE-TRUE-TRUE.

'Thanks to our friend Humphrey,
I don't think there will ever be
another fair like it,' he continued.

Everybody laughed, except Og
and me. I was still too tired to laugh.

Maybe Og was tired, too.

'So, for their great signs, their
terrific hamster hats, and their
special classroom pets, I'm awarding
the prize for best classroom spirit to

Room 26!' he said.

My tiny ears twitched with all the clapping and cheering that followed.

Then Mr Morales gave each student in Room 26 a free ticket for the bouncy castle.

As you can imagine, my friends were unsqueakably happy.

'Thanks, Humphrey,' Sayeh said.

'You're the best,' A.J. told me.

'You're Number One!' Miranda said.

Then my friends all left for castle bouncing and candy floss, for face painting and cakes.

I didn't have a ticket, but that was fine with me.

I'd had enough adventure for one day. I was ready for a nice long nap.

'Well, Og,' I said, right before I dozed off. 'Summer fairs are even more surprising than I thought. Don't you agree?'

My eyes were already closing when I heard a very loud 'BOING-BOING-BOING!'

My Creepy-Crawly Camping
ADVENTURE!

I'd like you to meet some of my friends

Og

a frog, is the other classroom pet in Room 26. He makes a funny sound: BOING!

Raise-Your-Hand-Heidi

is always quick with an answer.

Golden-Miranda

has golden hair, like I do. She also has a dog named Clem. Eeek!

Speak-Up-Sayeh

is unsqueakably smart, but she's shy and doesn't like to speak in class.

Stop-Giggling-Gail

loves to giggle – and so do I!

Repeat-It-Please-Richie

is Aldo's nephew and a classmate of mine.

Sit-Still-Seth

is always on the move.

Pay-Attention-Art

is a FUN-FUN-FUN friend!

I think you'll like my other friends, too, such as
Wait-For-The-Bell-Garth, *Lower-Your-Voice-A.J.*,
Mrs Brisbane and *Don't-Complain-Mandy*.

CONTENTS

The Great Outdoors

'What is the opposite of slow?' Mrs Brisbane asked our class one Friday afternoon.

Mrs Brisbane is the teacher in Room 26.

I am the classroom hamster.

I was thinking about the answer when Raise-Your-Hand-Heidi Hopper cried out, 'Fast!'

'That's correct, Heidi,' Mrs
Brisbane said. 'But you forgot to
raise your hand again.'

Heidi said she was sorry and Mrs
Brisbane continued.

'What is the opposite of happy?'
she asked.

A lot of hands went up.

My paw went up, too, but I guess
Mrs Brisbane didn't notice.

She called on A.J.

'Sad!' he shouted.

'Correct,' Mrs Brisbane said. 'But please Lower-Your-Voice-A.J. Now, what's the opposite of silly?'

'Eeek!' a voice cried out.

It was Gail.

She was almost always giggling.

That's why I call her Stop-Giggling-Gail.

But she wasn't giggling now.

In fact, she looked unsqueakably scared.

'What's the matter, Gail?' Mrs Brisbane asked.

Gail jumped out of her chair and pointed at her table.

'There's a spider!' she said. 'A creepy-crawly spider.'

'Ewww!' Mandy said.

Og, the classroom frog, splashed around in his water.

'BOING-BOING!' he said.

That's the way green frogs like him talk.

'Og likes spiders,' Richie said.

It was true. Og likes insects a lot.

He even likes them for dinner.
Ewww!

Mrs Brisbane walked over to Gail's
desk.

'It's just a tiny
little spider,' she
said. 'It won't hurt
you.'

I scrambled up
to the tippy-top of
my cage to get a better look.

The spider must have been tiny,
because I couldn't see it at all.

Mrs Brisbane put a piece of paper
under the spider and carried it across
the room.

Then she opened the window and gently let the spider crawl outside.

'Girls are scaredy-cats,' I heard A.J. whisper loudly.

'They're afraid of everything,' his friend Garth agreed.

I didn't think girls were scaredy-cats.

I didn't think girls were anything like cats.

I also didn't think I'd be afraid of a tiny spider.

Mrs Brisbane closed the window.

'Boys and girls, spiders won't hurt you. In fact, they can be helpful,' she explained.

I tried to picture a helpful spider.

With eight legs, a
spider could be a lot of
help when it came to
washing up and doing
other chores.

Mrs Brisbane said, 'They help get rid of pests. And they're very shy.'

'But they're creepy,' Gail whispered.

Then Mrs Brisbane asked, 'Back to my question: What's the opposite of silly, Gail?'

'Serious,' Gail answered.

You know what? For once she looked VERY–VERY–VERY serious.

*

At the end of the school day, Mrs Brisbane announced that Heidi would be taking me home for the weekend.

I'm lucky, because as a classroom hamster, I get to go home with a different student each weekend.

Og the frog stays in the classroom

by himself because he doesn't need to be fed every day like I do.

'Bye, Og!' I squeaked to my friend as Heidi carefully picked up my cage. 'See you on Monday!'

'BOING-BOING!' he replied.

I think Og wished he could come, too.

So did I.

★

'Humphrey, we're going camping,' Heidi told me in the car on the way home.

'Yippee! Where are we going?' I asked.

I hoped Heidi could understand me, but I know that all she heard was 'SQUEAK-SQUEAK-SQUEAK.'

'We're camping outside in the garden,' she said. 'It's supposed to be warm tonight.'

Maybe she understood me after all!

Once we got to the house, Heidi took me outside, behind her house.

Heidi's dad was there, hammering a stake in the ground to hold up a big yellow tent.

'Welcome, Humphrey,' Mr Hopper said.

'Thanks!' I squeaked.

I wanted to lend a helping paw but it's very difficult for a small hamster to put up a large tent.

Heidi set my cage on a table.

It was nice to feel the breeze in my fur and smell all kinds of interesting smells, like pine trees and roses.

After a while, I heard a familiar voice ask, 'Is Humphrey here?'

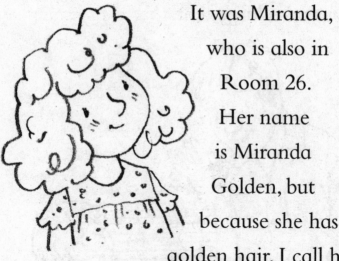

It was Miranda, who is also in Room 26. Her name is Miranda Golden, but because she has golden hair, I call her Golden-Miranda.

'We're having a camping night!' I squeaked.

Speak-Up-Sayeh, who is a quiet girl, was with Miranda.

'I'm so glad you can be with us, Humphrey,' she said in her soft, sweet voice.

Soon Gail arrived, too.

'Is Humphrey going to sleep outside in the tent with us?' she asked.

'Yes!' Heidi said.

'Eeek!' I squeaked.

I've gone to all kinds of houses and

flats on my weekend outings, but I'd
never slept outside before.

However, if my friends were
sleeping in the tent, then I would, too.

Stop-Giggling-Gail laughed
and soon everyone was having a
GREAT-GREAT-GREAT time.

Heidi's mum and dad cooked food
outside while the girls hit a ball back
and forth over a net.

When it was
time to eat,
Miranda and
Sayeh came over
to my cage and
gave me celery
sticks and carrots.

They were pawsitively yummy!

Then, the girls toasted marshmallows over the fire.

They looked ooey and gooey.

But they didn't look like something a hamster would like!

There was so much going on, I hardly noticed that it was growing dark outside.

'Look up,' Mrs Hopper said.

Pet hamsters don't spend a lot of time outdoors.

We spend even less time outdoors at night.

So when I looked up, I was amazed to see a sky full of twinkling stars.

We studied stars in school, but I

never knew they could be so bright.

As we all stared up, Mrs Hopper pointed out that some stars were grouped together and made little pictures.

It was unsqueakably hard to see the pictures at first.

'I see the Big Dipper!' Miranda shouted, pointing at the sky.

'I see it, too,' Gail said.

I stared and stared and then I saw it, too!

'That bright star is the North Star,' Sayeh said.

'And Mars is the red-looking planet,' Heidi's mum said.

I'd heard a story about green men

from Mars invading Earth, so I was a little worried.

But when I saw it shining, it looked like a very friendly planet.

Then Heidi's dad said, 'Let's go for a hike.'

'Where will we hike?' Heidi asked.

Mr Hopper smiled and handed each girl a torch.

'Right here in the garden,' he said.

Miranda put me in my hamster ball and set it on the ground.

'Let's look for night crawlers,' Mr Hopper said.

'What are they?' Heidi asked.

'Worms!' Mr Hopper replied.

'Ewww!' Gail said.

'They sound creepy and crawly,' Miranda said.

'Worms won't hurt you,' Mr Hopper explained. 'They help the soil.'

I crossed my toes and HOPED–

HOPED-HOPED he was right.

He handed the girls long sticks.
'You might have to dig around a
little to find them.'

I tried to stay close to the girls as I
rolled through the grass next to them.

Gail giggled nervously.

I was feeling a little nervous, too.

Then Heidi shouted, 'I found
some!'

All of us rushed over to the flower
bed where she was poking the earth
with her stick.

I was the last to arrive, because it's
not easy to roll a hamster ball on the
grass.

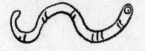 ★

When Heidi shone her torch on the dirt, Sayeh said, 'Ooooh!'

'They're creepy,' Miranda said.

'And crawly,' Heidi added.

Just then, my ball rolled up to the edge of the flower bed.

I agreed. The worms did look crawly and a little creepy.

They were slimy and slithery, too.

But they weren't scary.

'Creepy-crawlies don't scare me!' I squeaked, which made Gail giggle.

As my friends were busy shining their torches around the garden, my ball hit a little rock and made a sharp turn.

I started rolling away from my friends.

I wanted to stop but the ball kept on rolling.

I ROLLED-ROLLED-ROLLED past the tent and towards the house.

Ahead of me, I saw something very long and very skinny.

It reminded me of a worm, but it

was much bigger.

It was also bright green and it
curved all around, just like a snake.

'Eeek!' I shouted.

There was no doubt about it.

I was headed straight towards a
great big green snake!

Boys and Noise

I ran and ran inside my hamster ball, trying to steer it away from the snake.

Suddenly, I was blinded by a bright light.

'There you are, Humphrey!' Miranda shouted.

She scooped up my hamster ball and held it in her hand.

'THANKS-THANKS-THANKS!'
I squeaked. 'You saved my life.'

'Don't be afraid,' Miranda said.
'That's just the garden hose. It can't
hurt you.'

Whew! So the fur-raising snake
was really just a harmless garden
hose.

But I had to admit that creepy-crawly creatures were a little bit scary after all!

The girls decided it was time to go in the tent.

Miranda brought me along.

It was dark outside, but it was light inside.

There were four sleeping bags in the tent and a small wooden table.

Miranda put me in my cage on the table.

There was a tall electric lantern on the table and the girls had their torches.

Heidi taught her friends a funny thing called Morse code.

 She had cards with dots and dashes on them. The dots and dashes could be used to spell out words.

Then the girls would use their torches to flash each other messages on the tent ceiling by using long and short flashes.

The short flashes were dots.

The long ones were dashes.

Sayeh spelled the word 'hello'.

Heidi spelled the word 'camping'.

Miranda spelled a really l-o-n-g word.

I didn't know what it was because I didn't have a card.

Suddenly Gail shouted out, 'Humphrey' and everyone laughed.

I'd never seen my name in Morse code before.

Next, Heidi switched on a big box that played music.

Soon the girls were all dancing and acting silly.

I did a little dancing myself.

Dancing made me forget all about creepy-crawly creatures.

The music was LOUD-LOUD-LOUD.

But suddenly, I couldn't hear the music any more, because I heard a noise that was even louder.

It was a whooping, howling, laughing kind of noise.

It was coming from outside the tent.

'What's going on?' Heidi asked as she switched off the music.

'I think it's coming from Richie's yard,' Gail said.

Richie was also in Room 26 and he lived next door to Heidi.

The girls peeked out through the tent flap.

'Art and Seth are there with Richie,' Miranda said. 'And they have

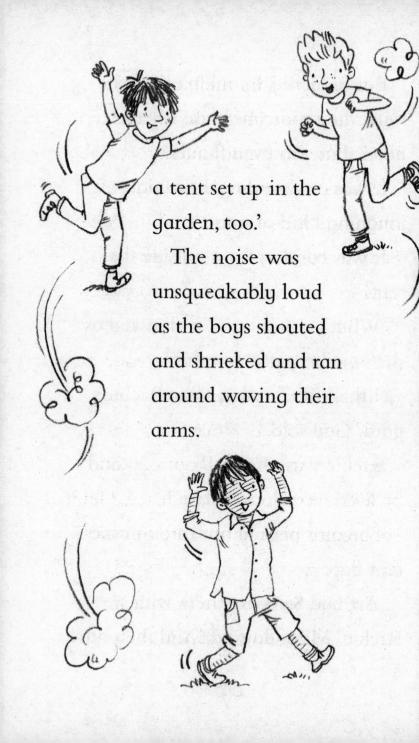

a tent set up in the garden, too.'

The noise was unsqueakably loud as the boys shouted and shrieked and ran around waving their arms.

Heidi turned up the music.

As the music inside the tent got louder, the boys got louder, too.

'That's it,' Heidi said, turning off the music. 'I'm going to tell them to be quiet.'

Miranda and Gail went outside with Heidi.

Sayeh took me out of my cage and gently held me in her hands.

'You come too, Humphrey,' she said.

When we got near the fence, Heidi shouted, 'Could you please be quiet? We're having a party over here.'

'And we're having a party over here,' Richie shouted back.

Then Art noticed me.

'Hi Humphrey,' he said. 'Why don't you come over here?'

'Yes,' Seth said. 'You're a boy, too. You belong here.'

It's true, I am a boy.

But Mrs Brisbane sent me home with Heidi for the weekend.

It was my job to stay with Heidi.

Art and Seth started making whooping and howling noises again.

'Aren't you girls afraid of the dark?' Richie asked.

'I know they're afraid of spiders,' Art said.

'We're not!' Heidi answered.

Then the boys started talking

about the bad things that might be
outside at night.

Art made
a scary face.
'Creepy-crawly
things,' he said.

'Howling,
growling things,'
Seth said.

'Ghost
and goblin
things,'
Richie said.
'Ooooo.'

Miranda folded her arms and walked up to the fence.

'Girls aren't afraid of anything,' she said.

'Right!' Gail, Heidi, and Sayeh agreed.

'Right!' I squeaked.

Hamsters aren't afraid of many things, except large, furry creatures with huge teeth like dogs and cats.

I'm not sure about the other scary things the boys described.

'Forget the boys,' Heidi said. 'Let's have some fun.'

*

Once we were back in the tent, Sayeh put me back in my cage again.

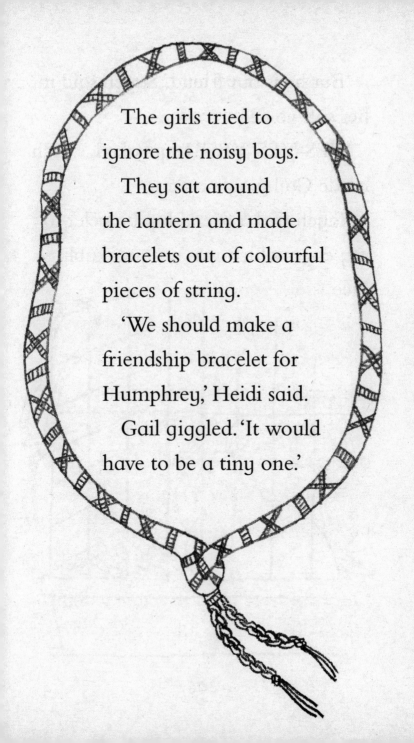

The girls tried to
ignore the noisy boys.

They sat around
the lantern and made
bracelets out of colourful
pieces of string.

'We should make a
friendship bracelet for
Humphrey,' Heidi said.

Gail giggled. 'It would
have to be a tiny one.'

'But he is our friend,' Sayeh said in her soft voice.

'YES-YES-YES!' I squeaked, which made Gail giggle again.

Sayeh tied a friendship bracelet to my cage, which was unsqueakably nice.

After a while, the boys stopped making noise.

It was nice and quiet.

Maybe it was a little too quiet.

'I guess the boys got tired,' Heidi said.

'Maybe they're afraid of the dark,' Gail said.

I heard some shuffling and whispering kinds of sounds.

'Something's out there,' Sayeh whispered.

'It sounds like it's near the tent,' Miranda said. 'Let's see.'

The girls quietly picked up their torches and tiptoed to the tent flap.

'There's something in the grass,'

Gail whispered.

'It's a ... great ... big ... snake!'
Heidi shouted.

'Eeek!' the girls screamed.

They raced towards the house,
leaving me all alone in the tent.

'Eeek!' I squeaked. 'Take me with
you!'

By then they
were too far
away to hear me.

So I did
what any small
hamster would do.

I hid in my bedding and tried to be
very still.

It wasn't easy, because I was

quivering and shivering.

Then I heard laughter.

I don't think snakes laugh, so I poked my head out of the bedding.

'Did you see those girls run away?' I heard a voice say.

It was Seth talking.

The other boys laughed.

I climbed to the highest point of my cage so I could see through the tent flap.

There was a snake outside.

It was VERY-VERY-VERY long.

It had a big pointed tongue sticking out of its mouth.

It was also very bright green.

And it wasn't moving at all.

I could hear the boys
laughing wildly.

'I didn't think girls could
run so fast,' Richie hooted.

'Or scream so loudly,'
Seth said.

Art howled with laughter.
'At a plastic snake! I
thought girls aren't afraid of
anything!'

Aha! So the snake wasn't
real.

It was a fake snake the boys
had placed in the garden.

'That's not nice!' I squeaked
but the boys were making too
much noise to hear me.

I was upset that the boys had
tried to scare the girls.

But I was HAPPY-HAPPY-
HAPPY that the long green
snake wasn't real!

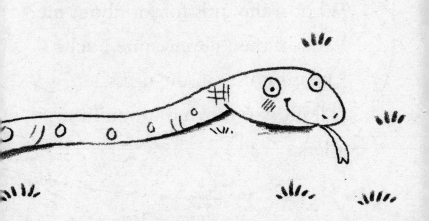

Out of the Shadows

Then it was quiet again.

I knew there wasn't a real snake in the garden, but I didn't like being alone in the tent.

What if the girls forgot about me?

What if they never came back?

I heard noises in the grass.

A light was moving around the garden.

I was about to dive under my
bedding again when I heard Heidi's
dad chuckle.

'So that's the problem!' he said.

I climbed up to the top of my cage
and looked out through the tent flap.

Mr Hopper was holding the plastic
snake in his hands.

'Girls!' he shouted. 'It's safe to come outside again.'

A minute later, Heidi and her friends appeared.

'Here's your scary snake,' Mr Hopper told them. 'It's made of plastic.'

'Those boys are awful,' Miranda said.

Heidi agreed. 'That was mean.'

'It wouldn't be a good camping night without a good scare,' Heidi's dad said. 'You'll be safe now.'

The girls returned to the tent and sat around the table again.

'I'm sorry we ran off without you,' Sayeh said. 'We were so scared.'

'Let's think of a way to get back at
the boys,' Heidi said.

'We could throw the snake back in
Richie's garden,' Miranda suggested.

'That wouldn't fool them,' Gail
said. 'It has to be something really
scary.'

The girls were quiet again as they
tried to think of a plan.

I tried to think of a plan, too, but I didn't really like thinking about scary things.

After a while, Heidi turned on the music again.

'Let's not let the boys ruin our fun,' she said.

Soon, the girls were dancing to the music and laughing happily.

Then, Heidi's
mum came out
to the tent.

'Time to
get into your
pyjamas and
brush your
teeth,' she said.

Heidi grabbed the big lantern as
the girls followed Mrs Hopper back
to the house.

After they left, it was quiet in the
tent.

It was lonely in the tent.

It was unsqueakably dark in the
tent!

Once in a while, I heard the boys

laughing and whispering from
Richie's garden.

'Girls!' I heard Seth say.

'Let's take the . . .' Then Art said
something I couldn't understand.

All the boys laughed.

Richie said, 'That will scare them!'

It sounded as if the boys were
planning to scare the girls again.

But since the girls weren't around,
they'd only end up scaring me.

As I sat there listening in the dark,
I noticed that Gail's torch was still on
the table.

I thought about the lock-that-
doesn't-lock on my cage.

Humans always think it's tightly

locked, but I have a secret way I can open it.

I knew it would be dangerous to be outside my cage, especially in the garden.

But if I could just flick on Gail's torch, the tent would be light and not so scary.

I twisted the lock and the door opened.

I headed straight for the torch, which wasn't very far away.

Getting to the torch was easy.

Turning the torch on wasn't easy at all.

There was a button on the side which I pushed and pulled.

The light didn't come on, so I jiggled it and joggled it.

I heard a little 'Click'.

Suddenly, light shone out of the torch.

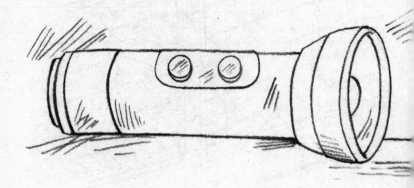

I felt much better, sitting in the big circle of light.

But as I turned to go back to my cage, I looked at the side of the tent.

To my alarm, I saw a very large, very shaggy, VERY-VERY-VERY scary thing.

'Eeek!'
I squeaked.

I raced towards my cage.

The scary thing raced across the side of the tent.

I turned and ran in the opposite direction.

The scary thing turned and ran in the opposite direction.

I stopped and sat still.

The scary thing stopped and sat still.

THUMPITY-THUMPITY-
THUMP!

My heart was pounding until I
realised that the scary thing was my
very own shadow!

I could hardly believe my eyes.

Who would think that a small
hamster like me could look so large
and scary?

I heard the boys scuffling outside
the tent.

'Sssh!' Art said.

'Sssh–sssh!' Richie said.

I knew they were planning
something creepy and crawly.

But maybe I could scare them first!

I stood in front of the torch and got

up on my tippy-toes.

Then I lifted my paws in the air
and opened my mouth wide.

I was happy to see that my shadow
didn't look like a hamster at all.

It looked like a huge and horrible
monster.

I looked like a huge and horrible
monster.

It was fun to look big for a change.

I opened my mouth even wider
and roared.

Of course, all that came out was
'SQUEAK-SQUEAK-SQUEAK'.

It was quiet outside.

I figured the boys hadn't seen my
shadow yet.

I needed to get their attention, so I
looked around.

Near me was the switch on the box
that made music.

I turned the switch and music
blared.

I pushed a little knob and the
music played louder.

I reached way up and pawed the

air like a scary monster.

And I crossed my toes and hoped
that my plan would work.

The Trouble with Monsters

'It's . . . a . . . monster!' Richie
shouted.

'Run for your life!' Art screamed.

'Help me!!' Seth shrieked.

They howled and yelled.
They shouted and screeched.

No matter how loud I screamed,
I could never sound as loud as those
boys did.

As I pawed the air and tried to
look big, I heard footsteps running
across Richie's garden.

'Help! Help!' The shrieks moved
toward Richie's house.

The garden was quiet again.

I relaxed and stopped acting like a
monster.

So, boys were afraid of some
things, too!

I hoped the boys weren't too
scared, but I was glad that my plan
had worked.

Then I heard footsteps coming

towards my
tent.

'Eeek!' I
squeaked.

I knew it
was probably
just Mr
Hopper, but I
didn't want to be caught outside of
my cage.

Then, my friends would find out
about my secret lock-that-doesn't-
lock!

And if they did, they might decide
to fix it.

Then I'd be stuck in my cage for
ever and ever!

So I made a dash for my cage and pulled the door closed.

'What's going on out here?' Mr Hopper asked.

He poked his head in the tent flap and looked around.

The torch was still on and so was the music.

My shadow was on the wall, but now it was my shadow inside the cage.

Mr Hopper laughed when he saw it.

'I think I see what happened,' he said.

He left and came back again with Heidi, Gail, Sayeh and Miranda.

'Are you sure it's safe out here?' Heidi asked. 'I could hear those boys screaming from inside the house.'

Gail nodded. 'I saw them running across the garden.'

'I'll show you what scared them,'

Mr Hopper said. 'Humphrey cast a shadow on the wall of the tent.'

He took them around the outside of the tent.

'It looks huge!' Miranda said.

'It looks like a lion in a cage,' Sayeh whispered.

'But it wouldn't scare me,' Heidi said.

'Me neither,' Gail agreed. 'Silly boys.'

The girls came back into the tent.

'I'm not afraid to be out here,' Heidi said.

'Girls aren't afraid of anything,' Miranda added.

'Girls aren't afraid of anything!' the girls all repeated.

'It's funny, but I don't remember leaving the torch on,' Heidi said. 'Or the music.'

Sayeh, Gail and Miranda didn't remember either.

I didn't squeak up and tell them I had turned them on.

The girls stood between the lantern and the side of the tent and made special shadows, like pictures on the wall.

Gail made a crocodile using her hand.

I was just a little bit afraid when
she snapped the crocodile's jaws.

Miranda made a bunny rabbit
with her hand.

It had tall, floppy ears.

Heidi made a dog using her hands.
She wiggled his ears and made his
mouth open and shut.

'Woof-woof,' she barked, which made Gail giggle.

'It's your turn now, Humphrey,' Miranda said.

I got up on my tippy-toes and raised my paws in the air, like a monster.

The girls saw my shadow and laughed and laughed.

I guess girls aren't afraid of anything after all.

When it was time for the girls to go to sleep, Heidi's parents came out to the tent.

Mrs Hopper tucked the girls in their sleeping bags.

I settled down in my bedding.

'Now, get some sleep, girls,' Mrs Hopper said as she left the tent. 'You too, Humphrey.'

★

Once we were alone, the tent was QUIET-QUIET-QUIET.

Outside the tent, things weren't so quiet.

First we heard something say, 'Whoo-whoooo.'

Gail sat up. 'What's that?' she asked.

'An owl,' Miranda answered. 'At least I hope it's just an owl.'

Then we heard a fluttering sound, like wings.

'What's that?' Heidi asked.

Miranda sat up and looked around. 'It's the tent flap,' she said. 'At least I hope it's the tent flap.'

It was quiet again – almost too quiet.

I was feeling a bit nervous, so I hopped on to my wheel.

Spinning always relaxes me.

I forgot that my wheel makes a loud whirring sound.

I don't notice it in the classroom, where there are other noises.

But in the tent, it sounded
unsqueakably loud.

'What's THAT?' Gail asked in a
frightened voice.

'I don't know.' Miranda sounded
even more frightened than Gail.

'It's just me,' I squeaked.

'Listen to Humphrey,' Sayeh said.
'He must have seen something.'

Heidi crawled out of her sleeping bag and stood up.

'That's it,' she said. 'I'm sleeping inside.'

'Me too,' Gail said.

'Me too,' Miranda said.

'And me,' Sayeh softly added.

'ME–ME–ME too,' I squeaked.

The girls quickly rolled up their
sleeping bags and took their torches,
the lantern and my cage back into
the house.

As Sayeh carried my cage across
the yard, I could see that the tent in
Richie's garden was dark.

I was pretty sure the boys were

sleeping inside.

And even though I didn't see any real creepy-crawly creatures in the garden, I was happy to sleep inside, too.

★

When Heidi took me back to school on Monday morning, Mrs Brisbane asked her how the weekend had been.

'Great,' Heidi answered. 'I had a camping night in the backyard with my friends.'

'So did I,' Richie told her.

'Oh,' Mrs Brisbane replied. 'Were you scared to sleep outside?'

'No,' Heidi said. 'Girls aren't afraid of anything.'

'Neither are boys,' Richie added.

They weren't exactly squeaking the truth, but I'm pretty sure they believed what they said.

During class, Mrs Brisbane asked, 'What's the opposite of frightened?'

Richie raised his hand and answered, 'Fearless.'

Later that night, I showed Og the friendship bracelet on my cage.

Then I told him all about our creepy-crawly camping adventure.

He splashed in his tank and said, 'BOING-BOING-BOING-BOING!'

'The girls were scared and the boys were scared,' I told my froggy friend.

'I wasn't afraid,' I said. 'At least not much.'

But I think that it's all right for girls and boys and even hamsters to be a little bit afraid of creepy-crawly creatures.

Even when the scariest thing in the garden turned out to be me!

Turn over for more
fun with Humphrey...

Dear friends,

Humans love their pets, and pets like me love their humans. I'm unsqueakably excited to share everything I've learned in Classroom 26 and beyond about the world of pets with you.

And hamsters aren't the only pets! Do you know how to look after a chinchilla? What is a puppy's favourite food? As well as learning top pet-care tips, you can tell me all about your pets in the special My Precious Pet section. I can't wait to meet them!

Your furry friend,

Humphrey

PET-tastic facts

WOOF!

LOTS of fun inside!

Humphrey's World of Pets

Betty G. Birney

Look out for my book of
unsqueakably funny jokes

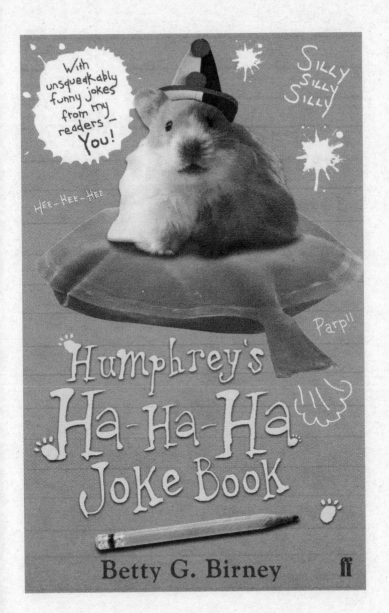

Or why not try the puzzles and games in my fun-fun-fun activity  books!

There's one
for summer . . .

Puzzles
and
Games!

Humphrey's
Book of
Summer Fun

ff

Betty G. Birney

. . . and one
for Christmas!

Ho, ho, ho!

Puzzles

Games!

Humphrey's
Book of
Christmas Fun!

Betty G. Birney

Humphrey and his friends have been hard at work making a brand new FUN-FUN-FUN website just for you!

Play Humphrey's exciting new game, share your pet pictures, find fun crafts and activities, read Humphrey's very own diary and discover all the latest news from your favourite furry friend at:

www.funwithhumphrey.com